BEVERLY CLEARY

HENRY AND THE CLUBHOUSE

Illustrated by LOUIS DARLING

HarperTrophy®
An Imprint of HarperCollins*Publishers*

Henry and the Clubhouse

Interior illustrations by Louis Darling

 Printed in the United States of America.
For information address HarperCollins Children's Books,
a division of HarperCollins Publishers,
1350 Avenue of the Americas, New York, NY 10019.

Library of Congress Catalog Card Number: 62-7161
ISBN 0-380-70915-5

First Harper Trophy edition, 2001

❖

Visit us on the World Wide Web!
www.harperchildrens.com

Table of Contents

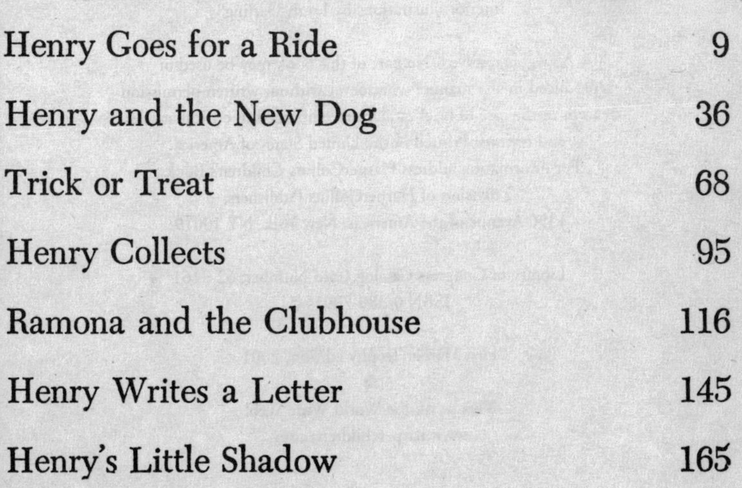

HENRY AND THE CLUBHOUSE

CHAPTER ONE

Henry Goes for a Ride

HENRY HUGGINS had a lot of good ideas that fall when he first had his paper route, but somehow his ideas had a way of not turning out as he had planned. Something always went wrong.

There was, for example, that Saturday afternoon in October, when Henry found himself with nothing to do until it was time to start delivering *Journals*. Naturally he wandered into the kitchen and opened the refrigerator to see what he could find. At the sound of the door opening, his dog Ribsy and his cat Nosy came running in case he should be planning to feed them.

"Henry, you just ate lunch," said Mrs. Huggins, who had washed her son's slacks and was now struggling to shove metal stretchers into the legs. "Can't you find something to do instead of opening the refrigerator every five minutes?"

"I'm thinking, Mom," answered Henry. He was thinking that he would like to build something, some kind of a house. A doghouse, a tree house or a clubhouse. A tree house would be pretty hard, but he was sure he could build a doghouse or a clubhouse. All he needed was lumber and nails.

"Well, think with the refrigerator door shut," suggested Mrs. Huggins with a smile. She had succeeded in stretching Henry's slacks and now she leaned them, tight on their frames, against the sink. "And *please* find something to do."

"O.K., Mom," said Henry, and walked out the back door in search of something to keep him busy. He considered. He could go over to the Quimbys' house and play checkers with Beezus, a girl whose real name was Beatrice, but her pesty little sister Ramona would probably spoil the game. He could go see if his friend Murph, who was the smartest boy in the whole school, was building anything interesting in his garage. Or he could try to sell subscriptions to the *Journal*. That was what he should do, but somehow Henry was not anxious to start ringing strange doorbells. No, what he really wanted to do was build something. He decided to scout around Klickitat Street and see if he could find enough boards for a doghouse. That would be the easiest to build and would not take much lumber.

As Henry walked around the side of his house, he noticed his next-door neighbor's car parked on the driveway with a U-Haul-It trailer attached.

Now that was interesting, thought Henry. What was Hector Grumbie going to haul?

The front door of the Grumbies' house opened, and Mr. Grumbie appeared to be coming out backwards. This was even more interesting. Why didn't Mr. Grumbie walk out frontwards? Bit by bit more of his neighbor appeared, and Henry saw that he was tugging at something.

Henry decided he had better investigate. From the Grumbies' front walk he discovered that Mr. Grumbie was pulling and Mrs. Grumbie was pushing a bathtub out of the house. They were sliding it across the floor on an old blanket.

Mr. Grumbie paused to wipe his forehead. "Whew!" he exclaimed. "These old bathtubs were built like battleships."

"May I help?" Henry asked eagerly. After all, his mother wanted him to find something to do.

"Sure," said Mr. Grumbie. "You can get on the other end and help push."

Henry ran up the steps, and because the bathtub was blocking the door, he climbed into it, out the other side, and joined Mrs. Grumbie in pushing.

Henry was secretly wondering, but was too polite to ask, if the Grumbies were planning to give up bathing. Instead he inquired, "What are you going to do with it?"

"Take it to the dump," answered Mr. Grumbie, "unless you would like to have it. We are remodeling the bathroom and have to get rid of it to make room for the new tub, which will be delivered Monday."

Henry thought it over. There were all sorts of interesting things he could do with a bathtub in his back yard. Wash his dog Ribsy in it, cool off in it himself on a hot day, bob for apples at Halloween. Build a clubhouse around it if he had that much lumber. All sorts of things. A bathtub in the yard would be much more fun than a tub in the bathroom, but Henry was sure his mother would not feel the same way about it.

"No, thank you, Mr. Grumbie," Henry said with regret and then he had a better idea. The new bathtub would come in a crate and perhaps Mr. Grumbie would let him have the boards to build a doghouse.

By that time several neighbors had come over to the Grumbies' to watch. Even Ribsy had taken an interest and had come down from the Huggins' doormat where he had been napping. Mr. Grumbie tied a rope around the tub and with the help of Henry and the bystanders who hung onto the rope, eased the tub, bump-bump-bump, down the front steps, slid it across the lawn, and then boosted it onto the trailer, where Mr. Grumbie tied it securely.

"Want to go for a ride to the dump?" Mr. Grumbie asked Henry.

The dump! Immediately Henry pictured a fascinating jumble of old bathtubs, washing machines, tires, and baby buggies. There was no telling what he might find at the dump. There might even be some old boards he could bring home.

"Can I ride in the bathtub?" he asked eagerly.

"Sure." Mr. Grumbie was agreeable. "Go ask your mother."

Henry ran to the open kitchen window. "Hey, Mom! Mr. Grumbie wants me to ride to the dump with him. Can I go?"

"All right, Henry." Mrs. Huggins' voice came through the window.

"Come on, Ribsy!" Henry bounded across the lawn and climbed into the bathtub. Ribsy scrambled in behind him.

"All set?" asked Mr. Grumbie, opening the door of his car.

"All set," answered Henry, and Mr. Grumbie maneuvered the car and trailer down the driveway and into the street.

Riding in a bathtub, which of course had no springs or upholstery, was bumpy, but Henry did not care. No one else in the neighborhood had ever gone for a ride in a bathtub. He shouted and waved to his friends Scooter and Robert, who were playing catch on the sidewalk. They stared after him in surprise. Ribsy put his paws on the edge of the tub and barked.

When Mr. Grumbie stopped at the first stop sign, Henry saw his friend Beezus and her little sister Ramona, who had a lot of string stuck to her chin with Scotch tape. Henry guessed she was trying to copy one of the many disguises of Sheriff Bud on television. Ramona never missed the Sheriff Bud program.

"Hi!" called Henry.

"Hello, Henry." Beezus looked with admiration

at Henry in the bathtub. He could tell she wished she could go for a ride in a bathtub too.

Ramona scowled ferociously and pointed straight at Henry. "Remember—only *you* can prevent forest fires."

Henry ignored Ramona. He knew she was only repeating what she had heard Smokey Bear say on television all summer. "So long!" he called to Beezus as Mr. Grumbie drove on.

Ribsy, tired of barking over the edge of the tub, curled up and tried to go to sleep, but whenever the trailer went over a bump, he lifted his head and looked annoyed. In the bathtub little bumps felt like big bumps. They rumbled and bumped down Klickitat Street to a main thoroughfare, and then Henry had an idea. He was the president of the United States riding in a parade! He sat up straight in the bathtub, nodding and waving and doffing an imaginary hat. Mr. Grumbie's car became a column of tanks preceding him down the

avenue, and one airplane in the sky became a formation of fighter planes overhead. Henry could practically hear the cheers of the throngs crowded along the curbs to watch his journey to the White House.

Henry did in fact hear a few real cheers, or perhaps jeers was a better word, mostly from boys along the way.

"Hey! Don't forget to wash your back!"

"Be careful! Don't step on the soap!"

With great dignity Henry nodded and waved. A great man on his way to the White House could afford to ignore such people, especially when he was surrounded by Secret Service men.

Henry was having too much fun to act dignified very long. He saw several boys standing in front of a bicycle shop and could not resist waving and shouting, "Hats off! The flag is passing by!"

"Boo!" yelled the boys. "Boo! Boo!" They held their noses and waved Henry on down the street.

Ribsy scrambled to his feet and barked over the edge of the tub. Henry, who was the kind of man who *would* take his dog to the White House, folded his arms and grinned in a superior manner, because he was riding in the bathtub and the boys were standing on the sidewalk. The afternoon had turned out better than he had expected, and he still had the dump to look forward to.

And then Henry passed a *Journal* truck heading in the opposite direction. Suddenly he was no longer president of the United States. He was no longer interested in lumber for a doghouse. He was plain Henry Huggins, a boy who had completely forgotten that he had forty-three papers to deliver this afternoon. This was terrible! If he did not get those papers delivered, his route might be taken away from him before he had had it a month. Then, because he was the youngest *Journal* carrier in the neighborhood, Mr. Capper, who was the district manager, and everyone else, would say he was not old enough to handle a route. And that would be about the worst thing that could possibly happen. He would never live it down.

"Mr. Grumbie! Mr. Grumbie!" yelled Henry, but Mr. Grumbie drove on down the street unaware that he was carrying his passenger farther and farther from his paper route.

"Mr. Grumbie! Mr. Grumbie!" There was no response but the bump and rattle of the trailer. Henry was trapped in a bathtub in the middle of Lombard Street. "Mr. Grumbie! Mr. Grumbie!"

At the next stop sign Henry stood up in the bathtub and frantically waved both hands, hoping to attract Mr. Grumbie's attention in the rear view mirror.

It worked, because Mr. Grumbie stuck his head out the window and called, "Something wrong back there?"

"My route!" yelled Henry. "I forgot my paper route!"

The signal changed and cars and trucks began to honk. Mr. Grumbie, in the center lane of traffic, had to drive on.

Henry sat down with a bump. The Saturday afternoon traffic was heavy and it would be difficult for Mr. Grumbie to change lanes while pulling a trailer. They were still in the center lane when they came to the next stop sign.

"I'll pull over as soon as I can," Mr. Grumbie called back to Henry.

Henry now felt ridiculous sitting in the bathtub in the middle of a heavily traveled street. He wondered why he had thought riding in a tub would be fun in the first place. A boy who was old enough to have a paper route was too old to do such a silly thing. Cross street after cross street went by and Henry was carried farther and farther from his route. By this time the other boys were counting and folding their papers and Mr. Capper was probably wondering what had happened to Henry, the youngest carrier. Maybe Mr. Capper was already wondering what boy could take over Henry's route. Maybe he was saying to Scooter and the other boys, "I'm afraid Henry isn't old enough to handle a route. Do you know any older boy who could take his place?" It was not a happy prospect.

A gap appeared in the right-hand lane of traffic and Mr. Grumbie eased his car and the trailer into it. There was a solid line of cars parked along the curb, and no place to stop. Another block went by. Still there was no place where Mr. Grumbie could stop. Henry caught a glimpse of a clock inside a dry-cleaning shop. Four thirty-five. He would never get to the district manager's garage and get his papers folded and delivered by six o'clock.

Mr. Grumbie signaled and made a right turn into a service station. Henry, followed by Ribsy, scrambled out of the bathtub as Mr. Grumbie got out of his car.

"I'm sure sorry I forgot about my route," Henry apologized.

"What are we going to do about it?" asked Mr. Grumbie. "I can't turn around and take you home now, because the dump closes at five and I've got to get rid of this tub this week end. Besides, I am renting the trailer by the hour and I want to get it back as soon as I can."

"That's all right," said Henry. "I have enough money for bus fare."

"Do you know the way home?" asked Mr. Grumbie.

"Sure. I can catch the bus across the street and I know where to transfer to the other bus." Henry was eager to be on his way.

"O.K.," agreed Mr. Grumbie, and climbed back into his car.

"Wait!" yelled Henry as Mr. Grumbie started to drive off. "Ribsy! Can you take Ribsy with you? I can't take him on the bus."

Across the street a bus pulled up to the stop,

discharged a passenger and departed with a puff of exhaust.

"I guess so. Come on, pooch." Mr. Grumbie opened the rear door of his car and Henry shoved Ribsy inside and slammed the door. He knew from past experience that a dog was not allowed on a bus unless it was in a box tied shut. Henry had enough problems without searching for a box.

When Mr. Grumbie drove off, Henry waited for the traffic light to change from red to green before he crossed the street to the bus stop. He had just missed a bus, he knew, and as he wondered how long he would have to wait for the next bus, he fingered the change in the pocket of his jeans. Bus fare and a dime left over. Enough for one telephone call. Probably he should call one of the boys and ask him to go over to Mr. Capper's garage and start folding his papers for him. But which boy? He had only one dime. What if he called Robert's house and Robert's mother answered and said he wasn't home? His dime would be gone.

Henry decided to telephone his own house and ask his mother to call Robert or Murph for him. Once more Henry waited for the traffic signal to change, ran back across the street and into the glass telephone booth in the corner of the service station. He pushed his dime into the smallest hole, dialed, and counted four rings.

"Hello?" It was Mrs. Huggins.

"Say, Mom," began Henry, his eye on the bus stop, "my paper route sort of slipped my mind and I wondered if you would phone Robert or Murph or one of the fellows and ask them to fold my papers for me. I'll get there as soon as I can."

"Henry, where are you?" asked Mrs. Huggins.

"In a filling station out on Lombard Street," answered Henry.

"It is twenty minutes to five now." Mrs. Huggins sounded exasperated. "You'll never get your papers delivered on time."

"Mom, I can't stand here all day arguing,"

Henry pointed out as a bus pulled up to the curb. "Here's my bus now!"

"Honestly, Henry, sometimes I wonder—"

Henry had to cut his mother off.

The traffic signal changed to red just as Henry reached the curb. "Hey, Mr. Bus Driver!" Henry called frantically. The bus driver glanced at him and pulled out into the stream of traffic. He had a schedule to follow and could not wait for one boy. Henry groaned and then he discovered it was not even his bus.

When the signal changed to green Henry walked across the street. He had done all he could do to get his route started and there was no use worrying about it. But Henry did worry. He wondered if his mother was able to find a boy to fold his papers and what Mr. Capper would say when the boy folded Henry's *Journals*. Henry worried when the bus finally came. He worried while he rode on what seemed to be the slowest bus in the world. He worried when he got off and waited for the second bus. He worried when he had transferred to the second bus, which seemed even slower. If there was ever a contest to find the slowest bus in the world, this bus would win. A snail could beat it any day.

And then as the bus finally reached Henry's neighborhood and drove down one of the streets on which Henry should have been delivering papers that very minute, Henry saw a car exactly like the Huggins' car. In fact, it was the Huggins' car. Henry could tell, because he saw his mother get out and throw a folded *Journal* toward a house. She threw awkwardly. The paper did not go far enough so she picked it up and threw again. Henry was horrified. A boy did not want to see his mother delivering papers, especially when she was such a terrible thrower. It was awful. He did not see how anybody could grow up and throw that way.

Hastily Henry jerked the cord that stopped the

bus at the next corner. He bounded out of the door and ran back to Mrs. Huggins, who was consulting his route book to see where to throw the next paper. Henry could not help feeling that he had reached her in the nick of time. He did not want

the passengers on the bus to see her throw again.

"Hey, Mom," he panted. "How come you're delivering my papers?"

"There wasn't anyone else to do it," answered his mother. "I couldn't reach Robert or Murph so I drove over to Mr. Capper's and found the other carriers were leaving with their papers. I've delivered twenty-eight of them."

"Gee, Mom, did you *fold* my papers?" asked Henry. If she had she was better at folding than throwing.

"The other boys had already folded them for you," answered his mother. "They must have known you were going to be late."

Henry opened the car door and pulled out his bag of *Journals*. "I'll take over, Mom," he said, as he slipped the bag over his shoulders. "Thanks a lot. You saved my life."

"You're welcome," answered Mrs. Huggins and then added, "I guess," as she climbed into the car.

Henry had to know something. "What did Mr. Capper say?" he called after his mother.

"He just laughed and wanted to know if I was taking over your route," answered Mrs. Huggins.

Henry wished he had his bicycle. He could actually cover his route almost as fast on foot, but it was more fun to deliver papers on his bicycle. Because he was short for his age the bag of papers bumped against his legs when he went on foot. He walked up one driveway and down the next, remembering which customer wanted his paper left on the doormat and which one had warned him against breaking the geraniums in the flower box on the porch.

Henry walked as fast as he could and soon covered his route. He was late, he knew, but with luck no one would complain—and so far he had been lucky. There was no reason why he should not continue to be. He was tired and sweaty when he reached home, but he was cheerful. The papers were delivered, weren't they? That was all that mattered.

When Henry opened the front door he was surprised to see his father wearing a white shirt and a necktie. Mr. Huggins always wore a sport shirt around home. "Hi, Dad. How come you're all dressed up?" he asked.

"Because your mother had quite a day with one thing or another around here, and we are going to take her out to dinner for a change," said Mr. Huggins.

"Oh—maybe I had better get cleaned up." Henry was surprised at this change in routine. He hoped they would not go to a fancy place with cloth napkins and a long menu. When he went out to dinner he liked to order a hamburger and pie.

"Well, Henry!" Mr. Huggins sounded stern. "Don't you have anything to say for yourself?"

"Why . . . uh . . . I finally got the papers delivered," answered Henry, not quite certain what his father expected of him.

"It seems to me your mother also delivered quite a few papers," said Mr. Huggins.

"Yeah, and golly, Dad, you should see her throw," confided Henry, demonstrating to his father the way his mother delivered papers. "It is pretty awful."

"Henry, I want one thing clearly understood," said Mr. Huggins, ignoring his son's remark. "That paper route is yours. It is not your mother's route and it is not my route. You are to deliver the papers and collect the money and do all the work yourself, and if you can't do it without any help from us, you will have to give the route to someone else. Do you understand?"

Henry looked at the carpet. His father did not often speak to him this way, and he felt terrible. He wanted his father to be proud of him because he was the youngest paper carrier in the neighborhood. "Yes, Dad," he answered. He felt he should offer some explanation for forgetting his route. "I was planning to get some old boards to build a doghouse."

Mr. Huggins grinned. "You don't need to build a doghouse. You're in a doghouse with your mother already."

Mrs. Huggins came clicking into the room on high heels. Henry caught a whiff of perfume and noticed she was wearing one of her best dresses, which meant a restaurant with cloth napkins. She looked so nice Henry felt ashamed of himself for criticizing the way she threw and for wanting a hamburger for dinner. "Gee, Mom, I'm sorry I caused you so much trouble," he said. "It just seemed like such a good chance to go for a ride in a bathtub that I just—well, I forgot all about my route."

"In a bathtub!" exclaimed Mrs. Huggins.

"Sure. Didn't you know? Mr. Grumbie had this old bathtub he was hauling to the dump on a trailer."

"A bathtub! I had no idea—" Mrs. Huggins sat down and began to laugh. "You mean you were riding down Lombard Street in a bathtub?"

"You told me to find something to do," Henry pointed out.

"Yes, I know I did," admitted Mrs. Huggins, "but riding around town in a bathtub wasn't exactly what I had in mind. Honestly, Henry, sometimes I wonder how you get into these things."

"I don't know, Mom, I just do," said Henry thinking with regret of the good idea that had somehow gone wrong. He knew one thing for sure. If he was going to keep his paper route he had better not get into things. He had better keep out of things—especially late in the afternoon.

CHAPTER TWO

Henry and the New Dog

HENRY soon found that there was not enough wood in a bathtub crate to build a really good doghouse. As he rode around the neighborhood delivering papers, he kept his eye out for any old boxes or packing cases that he could use. There was one empty house in the neighborhood which he passed every day hoping he would get some packing cases from the new owners, but the house remained empty. Wood was so scarce that he was about to give up the idea of a house for Ribsy when he had an unexpected piece of luck.

Most of the houses in Henry's neighborhood had been built way back in the nineteen-twenties when cars were shorter and narrower than they are today. Now many people were finding their new cars too long for their old garages and so they built box-like additions onto the ends of their garages to make them long enough for their cars.

One neighbor, Mr. Bingham, was not so fortunate. When he proudly drove his new car into his garage he found there was no way for him to get out of it. His garage was so narrow he could not open the door of his car. So poor Mr. Bingham backed out and parked his car on the driveway. All the neighbors on Klickitat Street had a good laugh over this, and Mr. Bingham announced that he was going to tear down his old garage and build a larger one.

As soon as Mr. Bingham began to tear down the garage, Henry rode his bicycle over to his house to ask if he could have some of the old lumber.

"Sure, Henry, help yourself," said Mr. Bingham, who was prying at a board with a crowbar. "Take all you want but get it out of here before Saturday, when the truck comes to haul it away."

"O.K., Mr. Bingham," agreed Henry. "Do you want to get rid of the windows, too?"

"Take anything you want," said Mr. Bingham.

Doghouse! Why, there would be enough lumber for a clubhouse, a clubhouse with windows and a good one, too. He would save up his paper-route money and buy one of those down-filled sleeping bags he had seen in the window of the sporting goods store and sleep out in the clubhouse he would build out of all the secondhand lumber.

Now Henry found himself with more to do than he had time for. He could not neglect his paper

route, so he saw that he would have to have help. He told his friends Robert and Murph about the free lumber and they saw the point at once.

"Sure, we'll help," they both said. The boys borrowed wagons and every afternoon between school and paper-route time they hauled lumber from Mr. Bingham's driveway to the Huggins' back yard. When Henry left to fold his papers, Robert and Murph went on hauling. By Saturday the boys were sure they had enough lumber for a clubhouse.

"Let's start building," said Henry eagerly.

"Nope," said Murph. "When you build a house, you've got to have a plan. You can't build it any old way."

"Aw, Murph," said Robert. "Where are we going to get a plan?"

Henry, too, was skeptical. He thought that any old way was the only way to build a clubhouse. "Yes, where are we going to get a plan?"

"I can draw one," said Murph. "I'll do it this week end. But remember, when we get the clubhouse built, no girls allowed."

"No girls allowed," vowed Henry and Robert.

"And when we get it built, we can sleep in it in our sleeping bags," added Henry, thinking to himself, when I get a sleeping bag. The boys agreed this was the thing to do with a clubhouse.

Mrs. Huggins looked at the old lumber in her yard and said, "My goodness, Henry, isn't that a lot of lumber?"

"Don't worry, Mom," Henry assured her. "The clubhouse will be real neat when we get it finished and I'll saw up the leftover boards for kindling."

Mr. Huggins looked at the old lumber. "I don't know about this, Henry. It looks to me as if you have taken on a pretty big job."

"The three of us can do it, Dad," said Henry, eager for his father's approval. "And I won't let it interfere with my paper route. Cross my heart."

"See that you don't," said Mr. Huggins. "If you can't handle them both you'll either have to give up your route or tear down the clubhouse."

That week end Murph, who was the smartest boy in the whole school and practically a genius, did draw a plan. He drew it on squared paper, each square equaling one foot. Henry was pretty impressed when he saw it and realized that Murph had been right. It would not do to build a clubhouse any old way.

Murph would not hear of building the clubhouse directly on the ground. "We don't want termites eating our clubhouse," he said.

Henry agreed that it would not do to have bugs chewing away at their clubhouse. This meant the boys had to buy some Kwik-Mix concrete and make four cement blocks for their clubhouse to rest on. It was soon plain to Henry that there was more to building a clubhouse than he had realized and that it was going to take a lot of time—time that he was not sure he had to spare because of his paper route. However, he could not back out now that Robert and Murph had already worked so hard on their new project.

Then one afternoon when Henry was folding his *Journals* on Mr. Capper's driveway with the other paper carriers, Scooter McCarthy spoke. "Say, Mr. Capper, I will be needing one more paper after this," he said.

"Is that so?" Mr. Capper sounded interested. "A new subscriber?"

"That's right, Mr. Capper." Scooter quite plainly was pleased with himself for having sold a subscription.

Henry suddenly pretended to be interested in a headline in the paper he was folding, because he hoped that if he did not look at Mr. Capper, Mr. Capper might not look at him. Henry was ashamed, because it was already October and he had not sold a single *Journal* subscription. Not that he hadn't tried—a little bit. He really had rung several strange doorbells before he became interested in the clubhouse, and had tried to sell subscriptions, but the results were discouraging. Strangers had a way of listening to his sales talk about the *Journal's* easy-to-read type with amused smiles and then saying, "No thank you." One man interrupted with a brusque "Not today" and closed the door in Henry's face. A lady embarrassed him by telling him what a splendid little salesman he was and then saying she couldn't afford to take another paper. Splendid *little* salesman! That was the last straw. After that Henry found it easy to think up excuses for not trying to sell new subscriptions.

Now Mr. Capper was saying, "Good for you, Scooter. Suppose you tell us how you went about selling the subscription."

"Aw, it was easy," boasted Scooter, stuffing his folded papers into his canvas bag. "I just told this man what a good paper the *Journal* was and he said he didn't have time to read it, because he went fishing every Sunday and I said, 'You could use it to wrap your fish eggs in,' and he laughed and said O.K., put him down for a subscription, so I did."

"I call that quick thinking on your part, Scooter," said Mr. Capper. "The rest of the boys could take a lesson from you."

Out of the corner of his eye Henry could see Mr. Capper looking around the group of boys. "What about you, Henry?" asked Mr. Capper. "You haven't turned in any subscriptions since you have had your route."

"Well . . . I—I have been trying," Henry said, admitting to himself that he really had not tried very hard. He had been much too busy with the clubhouse.

"I know it's hard to get started sometimes," said Mr. Capper sympathetically. "I'll tell you what you do. The other day I saw a *Sold* sign on a house on your route. When the new owners move in, you march right up to that front door, ring the doorbell, and sell them a subscription to the paper."

"Yes, sir." Mr. Capper made it sound so easy—march right up and sell them a subscription, just like that. "I'll try, Mr. Capper," said Henry, who knew the house the district manager was referring to. It was the house where he had once hoped to get enough old boxes to build a doghouse. It seemed a long time ago.

And so each day, as Henry delivered his papers, he watched for the new owners to move into the empty house. When he finally did see packing crates and empty cartons stacked on the driveway he decided he should give the people a little time, say about a week, to get settled before he marched right up and rang that doorbell.

The next afternoon Mr. Capper said, "Well, Henry, I see the new owners have moved into the empty house."

"I am going over today as soon as I finish my route," promised Henry, knowing he could not put off the task any longer.

When Henry had delivered his last paper he hung his canvas bag in the garage, washed his hands, combed his hair and, followed by Ribsy, walked the two blocks to call on the new neighbors. He did not ride his bicycle, because it seemed more businesslike to go on foot. Fuller Brush men did not ride bicycles.

As he approached the house he whispered to himself some of the things he planned to say. "Good afternoon. I am Henry Huggins, your *Journal* newsboy. I deliver the *Journal* to a lot of your neighbors." That much he was sure of, but he did not know what to say next. Find a selling point, Mr. Capper always said. Talk about some part of

the paper that would interest a new subscriber.

Henry walked more and more slowly. Ribsy finally had to sit down and wait for him to catch up. The *Journal* had a good sports section . . . a good church section. . . . How was Henry supposed to know what would interest a new subscriber? What if he told someone about the church section when all he wanted was to read the funny papers?

But before Henry could decide what to say, he met Beezus and her little sister Ramona. Ramona was wearing a loop of string around her neck. The ends of the string were fastened with Scotch tape to a cardboard tube.

"Hi," said Henry to Beezus. "What are you doing?"

"Keeping Ramona away from the television set," answered Beezus. "Mother says she spends too much time in front of it."

"Ask me my name," Ramona ordered Henry.

Henry could feel no enthusiasm at all for this new game of Ramona's. "What's your name?" he asked in a bored voice rather than risk Ramona's having a tantrum because he would not play.

Ramona held the paper tube in front of her mouth. "My name is Danny Fitzsimmons," she answered, looking down at the sidewalk and smiling in a self-conscious way that was not at all like Ramona.

"It is not," contradicted Henry. "You aren't even a boy."

"She's just pretending she's being interviewed on the Sheriff Bud program," explained Beezus. "That's her microphone she's holding."

"Oh," was all Henry could find to say.

"My name is Danny Fitzsimmons," repeated Ramona, smiling shyly in an un-Ramona-like way, "and I want to say hello to my mommy and my daddy and my sister Vicki, who is having a birthday, and Mrs. Richards, who is my kindergarten teacher, and Lisa Kelly, who is my best friend, and Gloria Lofton, whose cat just had kittens and she might give me one, and her dog Skipper and all the boys and girls in my kindergarten class and all the boys and girls at Glenwood Primary School and Georgie Bacon's sister Angela, but I won't say hello to Georgie, because I don't like him, and . . ."

"Oh, for Pete's sake." Henry was disgusted with Ramona's new game. "Why don't you just say hello to the whole world and be done with it?" He had no time for this sort of thing. He was on his way to sell a *Journal* subscription and get back to the clubhouse. "So long, Beezus," he said.

". . . and Bobby Brogden who has a loose tooth . . ." Ramona was saying as Henry went on down the street.

When Henry came to the house that was his destination, he turned to Ribsy and said, "Sit," not because he expected Ribsy to sit, but because he wanted to put off ringing that doorbell a little longer. He had not decided what to use as a selling point, because he could not even guess what might interest a new neighbor.

Ribsy sat a moment and then got up and sniffed at the shrubbery.

"I said 'Sit,' " Henry told his dog, deciding that it would be a good idea if Ribsy really did sit. Some people were very particular about dogs running through their flowers and he was anxious to make a good impression.

Like the good dog he was, part of the time, Ribsy sat once more, but he did not stay seated. He stood up and wagged his tail.

"Sit!" ordered Henry sternly, as he started up the steps.

Ribsy appeared to think it over.

"Sit!" Henry raised his voice.

Ribsy waved his tail as if to say, Do I really have to?

A strange dog, a Dalmatian, came trotting around the house and began to investigate Ribsy. The dogs sidled around one another, sniffing. Henry did not pay much attention. Dogs who were strangers to one another always did this.

Next a woman who was wearing an apron, and had a smudge of dust on her cheek, appeared on the driveway at the side of the house. She was older than Henry's mother. Probably she was old enough to be a grandmother. Before Henry had a chance to speak, the Dalmatian left Ribsy and frolicked over to his owner. Ribsy, an agreeable dog who was ready to play, followed.

That was Ribsy's mistake. Now he was trespassing on the Dalmatian's territory. The Dalmatian began to growl deep in his throat and to hold his whiplike tail stiff and straight.

Ribsy stopped short. This was his neighborhood. He was here first. It was the Dalmatian who was trespassing. Each dog began to resent the other's looks, sound, and smell.

"Ribsy!" Henry spoke sharply.

"Ranger!" The woman spoke sharply, too.

The dogs paid no attention to their owners. Each was too intent on letting the other know exactly what he thought of him. The growls grew louder and deeper and they raised their lips and bared their teeth as if they were sneering at each other. And just who do you think you are, Ribsy's growl seemed to say.

I have just as much right here as you have, Ranger's growl answered.

No, you don't, said Ribsy. I was here first.

I'm bigger, growled Ranger.

You're a bully, growled Ribsy.

Get off my property, Ranger told Ribsy.

You make me, Ribsy told Ranger.

"Cut it out, both of you," ordered Henry.

Planning to grab Ribsy's collar and drag him away, Henry jumped down from the steps to the lawn just as the growls erupted into snarls and the dogs went for each other's throat.

"Ranger!" shrieked the woman.

"Ribsy!" shouted Henry. The dogs were on one another in a twisting, tumbling tangle that seemed to be made up of feet, fangs, and tails.

Henry ran over to the snarling, yelping pair and just as he was about to grab Ribsy's collar, he found the other dog's mouth in front of his hand. Quickly he drew back. He saw that he could not stop the fight and since he could not, he wanted Ribsy to win. If it had not been so important for him to sell a *Journal* subscription he would have yelled, "Go get 'im, Ribsy."

"Look out!" shouted the woman. "Don't let him bite you!"

Neighbors began to gather on the sidewalk to watch the excitement. "Dog fight! Dog fight!" a boy yelled.

"The hose!" shouted someone. "Turn the hose on them!"

"I can't," cried the new neighbor. "I don't know where it is!"

"Hey, look at old Ribsy," said Scooter, who had ridden over on his bicycle to see what all the noise was about. "Go get him, Ribsy!"

"You keep quiet!" ordered Henry, even though he wanted to cheer his own dog on.

"Aw, your old mutt couldn't lick a Chihuahua," scoffed Scooter.

"He could, too," said Henry hotly. He w[illegible]

all sure Ribsy could lick a Dalmatian, but he could lick a Chihuahua. Henry was positive of that.

"Who's winning?" asked Robert, who had just arrived, along with Beezus and her little sister Ramona.

"The new dog," answered Scooter, and rode on down the street as if the fight was already over.

Half-afraid that Scooter might be right, because the new dog was both bigger and younger than Ribsy, Henry tried once more to reach into the snarling, rolling mass of dog to grab Ribsy's collar. He did not have a chance.

A man grabbed Henry by the arm and pulled him away. "Don't you know that's a foolish thing to do?" he demanded. "Those dogs might bite you."

"Yes, but he's my dog," Henry tried to explain. "I don't want him to get hurt."

The next-door neighbor was screwing the garden hose to the faucet. He turned on the water and advanced toward the dogs with the gushing nozzle in hand. "Stand back, everybody!" he yelled and turned the full force of the hose on the dogs.

Water sprayed in all directions. Still the dogs snarled and snapped. The man with the hose moved closer, so that the force of the hose was stronger. The stream of water caught Ribsy right in the face and blinded him for the moment. This gave Ranger the advantage. He seized Ribsy by the scruff of the neck, and though Ribsy was a medium-sized dog, Ranger began to shake him. The man turned the hose in Ranger's face.

Ribsy wrenched free and ran dripping down the

street with his tail between his legs, *ki-yi*-ing all the way. The Dalmatian was after him in a flash of black and white.

Henry did not know what to do—whether to run after Ribsy and try to rescue him, or to stay and tell the woman he was sorry his dog got into a fight with her dog, even though it was her dog that started it all. He also wondered what Mr. Capper would think of all this. A fine job of marching right up and ringing that doorbell this had turned out to be.

Before Henry had a chance to decide what to do, Ranger came trotting back down the street looking much pleased with himself. In the next block Ribsy could be heard *ki-yi*-ing toward home.

"Bad dog!" said Ranger's owner, shaking her finger at her pet.

Ranger shook himself with a great clatter of license tags. He did not look one bit sorry. Instead, he looked disapprovingly at Henry, who felt it was wise to retreat to the sidewalk. Ranger walked to the foot of the steps, flopped down, and looked around as if to say, I am monarch of all I survey.

Henry was still trying to collect his thoughts and say something. How had he planned to begin his sales talk? I am Henry Huggins, your *Journal* carrier, but what came next? Ribsy's *ki-yi*-ing in the distance did not help Henry to think.

Before Henry said anything, Ramona passed him and walked right up to Ranger's owner. "Are you the new lady?" asked Ramona.

"Why yes, I am, dear," answered the woman, pleased to have a little girl making friends with her so soon after she had moved into a strange neighborhood.

For once Henry was glad to see Ramona. If she talked to the lady a minute he would have a chance to think of his sales talk once more.

Ramona looked straight at the new neighbor. "Remember," she said with a ferocious frown as

she pointed her finger, "only *you* can prevent forest fires!"

Henry groaned to himself.

The lady looked startled. She had no answer for Ramona.

Beezus ran up to Ramona and grabbed her by the hand. "Don't pay any attention to her," she said apologetically. "She says that to everybody because she hears it on T.V. so much. You know,

Smokey Bear comes on and says it between commercials."

"Oh . . . yes." The lady did not look as if she understood at all. Perhaps she did not own a television set.

"Come on, Ramona." Beezus tugged at her sister's hand.

This was too much. Henry felt the only thing he could do was leave. First his dog got into a fight with the lady's dog and now the little sister of a friend of his practically accused the woman of going around setting forest fires. This was no time to sell a subscription. "I'm sorry about the fight," he blurted and left quickly, followed by Beezus, who was pulling Ramona along by her hand.

"Remember—only *you* can prevent forest fires!" Ramona shouted back to the lady.

That Ramona, thought Henry crossly. She was only five years old but she was the biggest pest in the neighborhood. At the corner Henry paused to glance back. The woman was nowhere in sight but Ranger was sitting on the front porch as if he was standing guard. It seemed to Henry that the dog was challenging him to set foot on his property. Just go ahead and try it, he seemed to say. Go on, I dare you.

To Henry's surprise Mr. Capper did not ask the next day if Henry had sold a newspaper subscription to the new neighbors, and Henry suspected Mr. Capper wanted him to bring up the matter. He didn't see how he could come right out and say, "I didn't get that subscription, because the new neighbor's dog didn't like my dog." Henry made up his mind that since he left Ribsy at home while he delivered papers, he would stop on his route this very afternoon and sell that subscription. By that time Ramona would be home watching television, so she could not spoil his sale a second time.

When all his papers were folded and stuffed

into the canvas bag, Henry mounted his bicycle and zigzagged down the street pitching *Journals* right and left. He was wearing a different T shirt today and he hoped the new lady might have been so busy watching the dog fight that perhaps she hadn't noticed what he looked like. "Good afternoon," he whispered to himself. "I am Henry Huggins, your *Journal* carrier. . . ."

When Henry came to the house he saw Ranger resting on the front porch, his nose on his paws, his eyes watchful. "Hi, Ranger," said Henry, in his most friendly manner.

Ranger's answer was to jump to his feet, barking furiously and leap down the steps after Henry.

There was nothing for Henry to do but pedal down the street as fast as he could go, with the dog snarling and snapping at his right foot every time he pushed down on the pedal. Never had Henry ridden a bicycle so fast. By the time he reached the corner he could no longer breathe in all the air he really needed to keep him going, and each time he bore down on the pedal he expected to lose a piece of his jeans or maybe even a piece of his foot.

By the middle of the next block Ranger suddenly stopped chasing Henry, turned around, and trotted toward home with an air of having done his duty. It seemed to Henry that the dog was not even out of breath.

Henry came to a stop, sat on his bicycle, and panted. Boy! That was close, but the worst of it was that Henry still had to deliver the papers in Ranger's block. When he had caught his breath he parked his bicycle against a tree and returned on foot very, very quietly, being careful to keep out of Ranger's sight. He did not throw the papers. He laid them silently on the lawns and tiptoed away so that he would not disturb Ranger. He had cured Ribsy from running off with newspapers by squirting a water pistol at him every time he went near a paper, but Ribsy was a good-natured dog. Henry did not think he would care to pause long enough to aim at Ranger. He might lose a leg while he aimed. He would like to see Mr. Capper march right up and ring that doorbell. He would have to wear a suit of armor. Or maybe even ride in a tank.

And each time Henry silently laid a paper on a lawn he became a little more angry. He had just as much right around here as that old Ranger. More, because he had lived here longer. And he was a human being, not a dog. By the time Henry had finished delivering the papers in Ranger's block he was just plain mad. He wasn't going to be pushed around by any old dog. No, sir! He was going to get that subscription if it was the last thing he did.

And remembering Ranger's speed and his sharp white teeth, Henry felt that getting that subscription might very well be the last thing he did.

CHAPTER THREE

Trick or Treat

HENRY HUGGINS was sure that this year he had thought up a better Halloween costume than anyone else in his neighborhood. No tramp or clown suit—not for Henry. He had thought up something different, something that no one else would think of in a million years.

There was just one flaw in Henry's anticipation of Halloween. He still had not sold the new neighbor a *Journal* subscription and although Mr. Capper had not mentioned the matter, Henry knew the district manager was waiting for him to say something about it. But what could Henry say? Every time he tried to approach the house Ranger chased him away. How the other *Journal* carriers, especially those in the eighth grade and high school, would laugh at that!

Henry was particularly worried because his father knew Mr. Capper, and if the two men happened to run into each other, Mr. Huggins would probably say, "How's Henry getting along with his route?" and Mr. Capper would answer, "He delivers the papers all right, but he's a terrible salesman." Mr. Capper always said there were three parts to a carrier's job: delivering, collecting, and selling. Then his father would say, "No more work on the clubhouse." He might even tell the boys to tear down the frame which they had so carefully built.

After supper on Halloween Henry tried to shove all this to the back of his mind. It was time to get ready to go trick-or-treating, a time for fun, not a time to think about his troubles. Henry went to his room and shut the door. He got out a bottle of ink (washable, it said on the label and he hoped the label knew what it was talking about) and an old lipstick of his mother's. He went to work and applied war paint to his face. When he finished he did not need a Halloween mask from the dime store like the ones the rest of the boys and girls would wear. No one would guess it was Henry Huggins under the lines and circles he had drawn on his face. Then he fastened an old belt around his head and through it stuck a feather from one of his mother's old hats. Next he draped an Indian blanket around his shoulders and fastened it with safety pins—lots of them. He needed his hands free to carry the paper bag for all the treats he would collect that evening.

Henry studied himself in the mirror and was pleased with what he saw—a fierce Indian that no one would ever guess was really Henry Huggins. But the best part of his costume was still to come. Henry opened his bedroom door. "Here, Ribsy," he called. "Come on, boy!"

Obediently Ribsy trotted down the hall and into Henry's bedroom. Henry opened a bureau drawer and took out a rubber wolf mask which he slipped over Ribsy's head. There! His costume was complete. He was now an Indian accompanied by a wolf, a funny-looking black-and-white-and-brown spotted wolf, it was true, but from the neck up Ribsy was a wolfish-looking wolf with long white fangs and a bright red tongue.

It would certainly be lucky for Henry if he and Ribsy happened to meet Ranger. Boy, old Ranger would take one look at Ribsy-the-wolf and practically turn a backward somersault he would be so surprised and scared. Then he would tuck his tail between his legs and run for home as fast as he could go with Ribsy-the-wolf right after him. By the time Ribsy got through with him, old Ranger would have learned which dog was boss around this neighborhood.

Unfortunately, as was so often the case, this good idea of Henry's had a flaw. With a rubber mask over his head Ribsy would not have a chance

f he got into a dog-fight because he would not be
.ble to bite back. With Ranger he probably would
ıot have a chance *without* a mask. It would be
visest for Henry to stay away from the new
ıeighbor's house that evening. He did not mind.
Halloween was no time to sell a newspaper
ubscription.

Ribsy sat down and scratched.

"Hey, cut that out!" ordered Henry. "You'll tear
he mask."

Henry went out to show off his costume to his
nother and father. Mr. Huggins laughed and Mrs.
Huggins pretended to be frightened at seeing an
Indian and a wolf in the house. Nosy, the cat, was
really frightened. He fluffed up his tail and
umped to the back of the couch, where he arched
his back and kept a wary eye on the wolf.

"Do you think Ribsy is going to stand for that
nask very long?" asked Mr. Huggins.

"I think so," said Henry as he opened the front

door. "We've practiced in my room every day thi
week. When I finished my route I came home an
put the mask on him. He seemed sort of puzzle
at first, but he's used to it now. I held him up so h
could see himself in the mirror, and I think h
likes it."

It was a perfect night for Halloween. The star
were bright and a north wind sent leaves skitterin
along the pavement. Jack-o'-lanterns grinned i
front windows. Bands of boys and girls, some o
them wearing costumes that glowed in the dark
trooped from door to door. Mothers of small chi
dren lurked in the shrubbery, while their littl
rabbits or ghosts climbed steps and rang doorbells
Henry felt so good he did a war dance in th
middle of his front lawn before he started dow
the street.

Before Henry had had time to ring a doorbell
he met a boy wearing a green cardboard head in
tended to look like the head of a man from oute

space. Suddenly the outer space man's eyes lit up in a fiendish and scary way that made Henry suspect his friend Murph must be inside. Murph was the only boy in the neighborhood who knew enough about electricity to think up such a costume.

Henry raised his hand in an Indian salute. "How," he said, carefully disguising his voice.

Silently the space man held out his hand. Henry grasped it. "Yipe!" he yelled, in his own voice, because he was grasping a buzzer that Murph held in the palm of his hand.

Murph laughed. "I thought it was you under that war paint." He leaned over and patted Ribsy. "Hiya, wolf," he said. "I knew who you were by your spots."

Together the boys proceeded down Klickitat Street ringing doorbells and shouting, "Trick or treat!" Everyone laughed at Ribsy's costume and gave Henry an extra treat for his wolf. Gradually their bags grew fat with candy, peanuts, popcorn balls, individual boxes of raisins, apples, and bubble gum. The boys no longer stopped at every house. They compared notes with other trick-or-treaters and soon learned which people gave jelly beans or all-day suckers. These houses they skipped. They did not like jelly beans and Henry felt that a boy who had a paper route was too grown-up to lick a sucker.

At one house which was completely dark, Henry and Murph hesitated. "Should we bother?" asked Henry. "It doesn't look as if the Morgans are home."

"We might as well skip it," said Murph, and just then a car turned into the driveway and drove into the garage. The headlights revealed a garage cluttered with tools and boxes, and decorated with a collection of old license plates. On a shelf at the back a stuffed owl with wings outstretched and claws poised for attack stared glassily into the night.

"Come on," said Henry, as Mrs. Morgan got out of the car. "She's got a lot of bags in back. Maybe she just bought something good at the market."

The two boys and Ribsy walked up the driveway. "Trick or treat!" shouted Henry and Murph. Murph pressed the button that lit up his outer space head.

"Oh, my goodness!" Mrs. Morgan exclaimed, turning around. "An Indian and a man from space. And a wolf! You certainly startled me." Then she hesitated. "Well . . . I'm afraid you will have to go ahead and play a trick." She peered into the paper bags in the back seat. "I've just come from the market, but all I bought was detergent and coffee and cat food and some things for breakfast. I don't have a thing to treat you with."

This was awkward. Henry could not recall a

Halloween when he had not been treated by everyone. Why, some of the younger children in the neighborhood did not know that trick or treat meant they were supposed to play a trick if they were not given a treat. Neither Henry nor Murph was prepared to play a trick. They had not even brought a piece of soap for soaping windows.

"Aw, that's all right, Mrs. Morgan," said Henry. After all, she was a very nice lady, and one of his *Journal* customers.

"Why, it's Henry Huggins!" exclaimed Mrs. Morgan. "I didn't recognize you in all that war paint."

Naturally Henry was pleased that his neighbor had not penetrated his disguise. "That's a keen owl you have there," he remarked. "It's real fierce-looking, as if it was about to catch an animal or something."

"It's a great horned owl," said Murph, whose

head was full of information like this. "Those license plates go all the way back to 1929."

"Mr. Morgan always nails the old plates on the wall every time he gets a new one." Mrs. Morgan followed Henry's eyes to the owl. "Henry—since I don't have a treat for you, how would you like to have the owl?" she asked, as if she had just had an inspiration.

"Gee, Mrs. Morgan . . ." Henry was almost speechless, he was so busy considering the possibilities of a stuffed owl. In his room on his chest of drawers . . . or in the clubhouse. That was it! In the clubhouse. A stuffed owl was exactly what they needed for a finishing touch. "Gee, could I really have it?"

"Certainly," said Mrs. Morgan. "You boys just climb up on that apple box and lift it down."

The boys quickly obeyed before Mrs. Morgan could change her mind. Henry could scarcely believe his good fortune. The owl was at least five feet from wing tip to wing tip. Why, this was better than all the peanuts and popcorn balls in the world. "Thanks, Mrs. Morgan," said Henry. "Thanks a lot."

"Oh, don't thank me," said Mrs. Morgan. "I've been looking for a way to get rid of that thing for years. It's too big to go into the garbage can, and the Goodwill refused to take it."

"Are you going to put it in the clubhouse?" asked Murph, when the boys had left Mrs. Morgan's garage.

"Sure," said Henry. "Then we can call it a hunting lodge."

"Nobody hunts owls," Murph pointed out.

Henry could see no reason for continuing the rounds of the neighborhood. Nothing he would get could possibly be as good as a stuffed owl. Besides, carrying his paper bag and lugging his owl, which was an awkward size and shape, did not leave him a free hand for ringing doorbells.

On their way home Henry and Murph met a gypsy and a small red devil who turned out to be Beezus and—appropriately, Henry felt—Ramona. They were carrying a jack-o'-lantern that had been carved too long before Halloween. Now its lips were shriveled and there was a smell of cooking pumpkin in the air.

"A stuffed owl!" exclaimed Beezus. "How spooky! What are you going to do with it?"

"Put it in the clubhouse," said Henry, "but no girls are allowed." Henry really would not have minded Beezus' visiting the clubhouse, but Murph had been firm from the beginning. No girls allowed. And perhaps Murph was right. A boy who was in the business of delivering papers was too old to play with girls.

Before Beezus could answer, Ramona held up

her paper bag. "We each got a Nutsie," she said and began to recite. "Nutsies give both children and adults quick energy. Avoid that mid-afternoon slump with a Nutsie, chock-full of protein-rich nuts!"

"Jeepers," said Henry. "What does she do? Memorize commercials?"

"Oh, Ramona," said Beezus impatiently, "stop reciting commercials. You don't have to believe things just because you hear them on T.V." Then she turned to Henry and Murph. "Stay away from that house on the corner," she advised. "When we said, 'Trick or treat' they said they would like to see us do a trick for them and why didn't we sing a little song. I guess they don't understand about Halloween."

"I sang a little song," boasted Ramona, twitching her red devil's tail. "I sang 'Crispy Potato Chips are the best, North or South, East or West, Crispy Chips, hooray, hooray! Get your Crispy Chips today.' "

"And the people thought it was cute," said Beezus crossly. "They asked her to do it again each time."

"It's a nice song," said Ramona. "I like it."

While they were standing under the street light, Scooter McCarthy appeared out of the darkness. He was wearing his father's old Marine uniform, without even a mask, and was licking a candy apple. "Hey, where did you get the owl?" he asked.

"Mrs. Morgan," answered Henry, who suspected Scooter of wanting to let everyone know that his father had been a Marine.

Scooter looked closer. "Sort of beat-up, but not bad," he conceded.

"Where did you get the candy apple?" asked Murph.

"That house where the people moved in last week."

"What are we waiting for?" Murph asked Henry. "Come on, let's get some candy apples."

"Oh . . . I don't know." Henry did not think he cared to meet Ranger when he was wearing an Indian blanket and carrying a stuffed owl. He might trip if he tried to run. There was Ribsy to think of, too. Henry did not want his dog to get in another fight with Ranger.

"Henry is scared of their dog," said Scooter.

"I am not!" said Henry indignantly.

"Then why do you let him chase you every day?" asked Scooter.

Henry wondered how Scooter knew about this. "Come on, Murph, let's go ring the new lady's doorbell." Henry spoke with more assurance than he felt. He only hoped that the dog would feel more friendly toward him when he was not delivering papers and perhaps would not even recognize him in his war paint. Ranger would probably be in the house and, anyway, Henry was not going to be pushed around by a dog. If his owner was giving out candy apples, Henry was going to have a candy apple. If the worst came to the worst he could use the owl to fend off Ranger. He also had the happy thought that it might be pretty hard for Ranger to bite him through the folds of a blanket.

"Sit, Ribsy," Henry ordered, when they were in front of the house. To be on the safe side he pulled off the rubber wolf mask. "Sit!" he said again.

For once Ribsy sat. Probably he was no more eager to meet Ranger than Henry was. As the boys advanced toward the front steps Henry noted that the wind was blowing his scent away from the house. He also thought that since he was disguised with war paint the lady would not recognize him as the boy whose friend had told her that only she could prevent forest fires. That was a good thing. "You ring," he said to Murph, as he rested his bag of treats in front of his feet and held the owl in his left hand. This left his right hand free to accept the candy apple.

Murph turned on his outer-space eyes and rang the doorbell while Henry braced himself. The door opened and the new neighbor, the one to whom Henry was so anxious to sell the *Journal,* appeared.

"Oh!" She clapped her hands to her chest and stepped back, pretending great fright.

"Trick or treat!" shouted Henry and Murph, who could not help being pleased by her performance. Henry was glad that the lady could not possibly recognize him.

Ranger, who was trotting toward the door, saw the owl with its outstretched wings, sharp claws and glittering eyes, looking as if it were about to attack. He skidded to a stop on the hardwood floor, turned, and tried to run, but his claws could not dig into the slippery wood. He slipped and skidded to the edge of the carpet, where his claws could take hold. He slunk under the chair, whimpering with fright.

Old Ranger wasn't so brave after all, Henry thought, as he heard a growl behind him in the

dark. Now that Ranger had turned tail, Ribsy was ready to protect his master.

"Go home!" Henry ordered even though he could not see Ribsy.

The lady bent over and looked under the chair. "What's the matter with Ranger?" she asked. "What's the matter with the boy? Come on out, baby. It's just a stuffed owl. It can't hurt you."

Baby! The lady called that ferocious animal "Baby!" Henry heard the jingle of license tags behind him. He noticed that Ranger had heard them too. Henry wished he had not bothered with a candy apple when he already had a whole bag full of things his mother would not want him to eat.

At that moment Ribsy poked his head around the door.

"Why, it's that dog that got into the fight with Ranger," exclaimed the lady, holding out a tray of candy apples to Henry, "and you must be the paper boy."

Henry accepted an apple. "Uh . . . yes," he admitted now that his disguise had been penetrated. He used his foot to give Ribsy a shove down the steps. "I—I'm sorry about the fight and what Ramona said about not causing forest fires."

"Oh, children and pets!" said the lady, with an airy laugh. "You never can tell what little children are going to say, and I have had a lot of pets and they are always into something. Don't worry about the little girl and please don't worry about Ranger. He'll get over it."

Suddenly a word the woman had spoken repeated itself in Henry's mind. Pets. She was interested in pets! He looked at Ranger whimpering under the chair, steadied his owl, and decided to speak up. Now that the lady knew who he was he had nothing to lose, and somehow he had a feeling it would be easier when he was disguised as an Indian. It was almost as if someone else was speaking instead of Henry. "My name is Henry Huggins," he began. "I am your *Journal* carrier. I deliver the *Journal* to many of your neighbors. The Sunday supplement has a good column about pets you might enjoy reading. . . ." Here he paused to catch his breath, and try to think what to say next.

"Well, it's about time," said the lady with a smile. "I am Mrs. Peabody, and I have been waiting for you to come and sell me a subscription."

"You have?" This possibility had never occurred to Henry.

"Yes, I thought you might want to get credit for selling a subscription," answered Mrs. Peabody.

"Oh, he does," Murph assured her earnestly.

"It took you so long I was about to give up and phone the paper myself," Mrs. Peabody continued.

"Please don't do that," said Henry, lest the lady change her mind about the subscription.

"I won't," Mrs. Peabody assured him. "I have a grown son who used to deliver papers when he was your age and I know all about it."

Henry wondered if she really did know everything about a paper route—things like dogs who chased paper boys. Ranger, it seemed to him, was getting over his scare. He had poked his nose out from under the couch.

"Now don't you worry about my dog," said the lady a second time. "He felt he had to defend his property against intruders, but now that he sees we are friends, he will be all right." She leaned over and spoke to her dog. "Won't you, Ranger, baby?"

Ranger peered out from under the couch and thumped his whiplike tail.

"He's really just a lamb," said Ranger's owner.

Some lamb, thought Henry, but he felt that he should try to make friends with Ranger, so he gave Ribsy another shove with his foot and said, "Hiya, Ranger? How's the fellow?"

Ranger did not growl or bare his teeth. That was progress.

"Well . . . uh . . . thanks a lot for the subscription and the candy apple," said Henry. "I'll start leaving the paper tomorrow."

"Good!" said Mrs. Peabody. "I've missed the crossword puzzle."

She did not say one word about having the paper left in some special place, not a word about being careful not to hit the shrubs or the windows.

Henry could tell this lady was going to be a good customer. Probably she would always be home when he came to collect and would always have the exact change ready.

"Good night, Harry," the lady called after him. She was such a nice lady Henry did not want to tell her his name was Henry, not Harry.

"Well, what do you know," Henry remarked to Murph when they were out on the sidewalk once more. "Two treats—a candy apple and a *Journal* subscription." He felt as if a burden had been taken from him. He had actually sold a subscription, and now that he had sold one, he was sure he could sell others. From now on it would be easy.

Murph laughed. "The way that old Ranger dived under that couch! He sure thought something was after him, but he didn't know what."

Henry laughed too. He laughed at the thought of Ranger skidding on the floor. He laughed because he felt good.

"I've had enough," said Murph. "Let's go home."

"Not yet," said Henry, who no longer felt like going home. "Just one more house."

"What for?" asked Murph. "We have more junk than we can eat now."

"Aw, come on, Murph," coaxed Henry. "Let's stop at Mr. Capper's. I'll bet he's giving something good."

"You just want to tell him about the subscription," said Murph.

"Yup," answered Henry. It was true. News like this could not wait until tomorrow. Now it would be safe for his father to talk to Mr. Capper, who would tell him Henry was a good salesman. There was no danger of his father's telling him to tear down the clubhouse now.

"O.K.," agreed Murph, and the boys started toward Mr. Capper's house with the good news.

CHAPTER FOUR

Henry Collects

The day after Halloween was the first of November. Henry regretfully had to leave the building of the clubhouse to Robert and Murph, while he called on his subscribers to collect for the *Journal.*

Beezus visited the Huggins' back yard and offered to pound nails in Henry's place. "Ramona is playing over at Lisa's house," she said, "so she won't get in the way."

Murph scowled. "No girls allowed."

"Oh, all right," said Beezus, and flounced down the driveway.

"It won't take me long to collect," said Henry cheerfully, but it was not long before his cheerfulness faded. First of all, he started out to collect without taking any money along. He had to go home and rob his piggy bank so he would have change to give his customers. That took time.

As usual, Henry found that not everyone was home when he rang the doorbell. Sometimes he had to go back a second and even a third time. That took more time. One man who was home had only a twenty-dollar bill. Henry did not have that much change, so he had to make a second trip. And all the time he was eager to get back to the clubhouse.

Henry did have one customer who was just about perfect to collect from. That was Mrs. Peabody. She not only had the exact change ready, she had it waiting on a table by the front door so that Henry was not delayed while she went to get her purse. She also had some cookies wrapped in a paper napkin for him. Ranger behaved himself, too. He watched Henry, but he did not move.

There was only one thing wrong with Mrs. Peabody. She opened the door and said, "Well, here is Harry Higgins to collect for the paper!"

Naturally, since she was such a good customer to collect from, Henry did not like to speak up and say, "Excuse me, my name is Henry Huggins." He just gave her the receipt and thanked her for the cookies.

"You're welcome, Harry," said Mrs. Peabody.

Harry Higgins! Henry wondered how Mrs. Peabody would feel if he started calling her Mrs. Beanbody, not that he intended to. Now that Ranger behaved himself, Mrs. Peabody was his nicest customer, and he would never hurt her feelings.

Then in contrast to Mrs. Peabody there was

Mrs. Kelly, who was Henry's most difficult customer when it came to collecting. The first time Henry walked up the Kellys' walk, which was strewn with tricycles, kiddie cars, and battered kitchen utensils, and rang the doorbell, a little voice inside screamed, "Doorbell, Mommy!"

Mrs. Kelly called from an upstairs window, "Who is it?"

"It's me, Henry Huggins," Henry answered. "I'm collecting for the *Journal.*"

"You'll have to come back some other time," Mrs. Kelly called down. "I'm giving the baby a bath."

The second time Henry rang the doorbell, Mrs. Kelly answered. She wore pedal pushers and an old blouse, and her hair was bound up in a faded scarf. Two small children followed her to the door, and another was crying somewhere in the house. Behind Mrs. Kelly, Henry caught a glimpse of Ramona playing with a little girl her own age.

"Oh, it's you again," said Mrs. Kelly, before Henry had a chance to speak. "I'm sorry. I don't have a cent in the house. You'll have to come back after payday."

Henry realized as he tripped over an old muffin tin on his way down the front steps that he had forgotten to ask Mrs. Kelly when payday was.

Henry was able to drive quite a few nails into the clubhouse before he got up his courage to go back to the Kellys'. The building, under Murph's direction, was going along smoothly when it was not interrupted by Ramona, who was sometimes accompanied by Lisa, her little friend from kindergarten. They wanted to know if they could have nails to take home. They also asked the same riddles over and over.

"How is a dog different from a flea?" Ramona would ask.

"I don't know." Henry was the only boy who bothered to answer.

"Because a dog can have fleas, but a flea can't have dogs," Ramona would answer, and no matter how many times she asked the riddle, she and Lisa screamed with laughter at the answer.

"What is black and white and red all over?" Ramona always asked next.

"No girls allowed!" Murph yelled at this point. Then Ramona and Lisa would walk down the driveway, scuffing the toes of their shoes on the cement to show they were angry. The next day they would be back.

"Can't you find a way to get rid of those pesty girls?" Murph asked.

Henry could only shrug. There was no easy way to get rid of Ramona.

Finally Henry decided he had to get up his courage to go back to the Kellys', or Mr. Capper would start asking him why he had not finished collecting.

This time Mrs. Kelly met him at the door with a baby balanced on her hip. "Oh, it's you again," she said for a second time, glancing over her shoulder toward the kitchen, where Henry could hear an automatic washing machine running. "Come in while I find my purse."

Henry stepped into the living room, which was scattered with toys, children's clothing, and crumpled pages torn from magazines. There was a bowl of soggy breakfast food on the coffee table.

A little boy who was sucking his thumb and holding an egg beater looked out of the kitchen door.

"Don't pinch your fingers in the egg beater, Kermit," said Mrs. Kelly. She looked wearily at Henry. "Would you mind keeping an eye on the children while I go find my purse? They are all in the kitchen. Kermit, Bobby, Lisa, and her little friend."

"Sure." What else could Henry say? Anything to collect and get back to his clubhouse. He stepped into the kitchen where the washing machine was busily swish-swashing. Lisa and her little friend, who turned out to be Ramona, were kneeling on chairs at the kitchen table, cutting circles out of Play-Doh with cookie cutters.

"I know him," said Ramona to Kermit and Bobby. "That's Henry Huggins."

"Let's cross him out," suggested Lisa. Laughing wildly, the two little girls made big crisscross motions in the air in front of Henry.

"There," said Ramona. "I guess we crossed him out."

Henry did not know what to make of this and did not have time to give the matter much thought, because Bobby started to crawl out of the kitchen. Henry did not know how old Bobby was, but he knew he couldn't be very old, because he was wearing diapers, plastic pants, and a T shirt. In one hand he carried a piece of toast. Henry had never seen a baby drool as much as Bobby. As he crawled he left little puddles on the floor.

Henry heard Mrs. Kelly's footsteps going up the stairs. Bobby dropped his toast on the floor. Lisa and Ramona giggled over some private girl joke. Kermit spun the egg beater and made a noise like machinery with his mouth. The washing machine churned. A dog walked into the kitchen, picked up Bobby's toast, and dropped it again. It did not look as if anyone would get into trouble, but just the same Henry hoped their mother would hurry back. He was a paper carrier, not a baby sitter.

Bobby picked up the soggy toast the dog had dropped and began to chew it. "Hey," said Henry feebly. He was pretty sure babies were not supposed to eat toast that had been in a dog's mouth. Gently he tried to take the toast from Bob, who clung to his crust and uttered a piercing scream. Henry backed away. Bobby put the toast back in his mouth and gnawed contentedly. Oh well, thought Henry, it looks like a pretty clean dog.

Then Henry discovered Kermit was missing. He stepped into the living room where Kermit was twirling the egg beater in time to see the dog lap up the soggy breakfast food in the bowl on the coffee table. "Cut that out," said Henry even though it was too late to do any good.

The washing machine stopped swish-swashing and was silent as if it was resting up before starting to spin.

Mrs. Kelly called down from upstairs, "Kermit, what did you do with my purse?"

"I put it under the bed so Bobby wouldn't get it," answered Kermit.

Henry heard a chair being dragged across the kitchen floor. Followed by Kermit and the dog he went back to investigate. Ramona was standing on a chair in front of the washing machine. She was not actually doing anything wrong, but knowing her, Henry was not taking any chances. "You better get down from there," he said.

"Pooh," said Ramona.

The washing machine gave a loud click and started to spin. Ramona reached toward the lid.

"What do you think you're doing?" Henry spoke more forcefully this time.

"I don't have to mind you," Ramona informed him. "You're just an old boy." She lifted the lid of the washing machine to peek inside. Instantly dirty water and detergent spun out of the machine with a great *whoosh,* hitting Henry right in the face, drenching Ramona and spraying the whole kitchen.

"Cut that out!" yelled Henry, snatching Ramona off the chair and slamming down the lid of the washing machine, but not until the jet of dirty water had circled the kitchen several more times.

All the children were howling with fright and Ramona howled the loudest. The dog shook himself and began to bark. Henry mopped his face with his damp sleeve and looked around at the rivulets of dirty water trickling down the walls and cupboard doors onto the floor. It was a wet, sloppy mess, and there was no time to clean it up. "What did you have to go do that for?" he demanded of Ramona, as Mrs. Kelly's feet came thumping down the stairs.

Ramona who was dripping with dirty water

stopped howling and looked sulky. "I just wanted to see what it looked like inside when it was spinning," she said.

Disgusted as he was, Henry felt a small flash, a very small flash, of understanding for Ramona. He had always been curious to see a load of spinning clothes, too.

"Oh, my goodness!" exclaimed Mrs. Kelly from the doorway as she looked at the wet children and dripping walls. The children's howls subsided when they saw their mother. "What on earth happened?"

"I'm awfully sorry," Henry apologized. "I tried to stop Ramona, but she lifted the lid of the washing machine before I could get to her." He glared at Ramona, who made a face right back at him.

"Tattletale," said Ramona.

Maybe he was a tattletale, but Henry didn't know what else he could have told Mrs. Kelly. She would know the washing machine did not open itself. "I'll help wipe it up," he offered, feeling this was the least he could do.

Mrs. Kelly looked around her dripping kitchen. "Oh well," she said with a sigh. "I suppose I should wash down the walls sometime. No, don't bother to help. You just take Ramona home so she can get cleaned up and into some dry clothes."

"O.K. . . ." Henry tried to sound willing. "I'm sure sorry, Mrs. Kelly. I'd be glad to come back and help clean up."

Mrs. Kelly managed a smile. "No thank you, Henry. You've done enough already."

Henry was not at all sure how she meant this remark. "Come on, Ramona," he said, anxious to get away.

Outside, Ramona pushed her wet hair back from her forehead so it wouldn't drip into her eyes and said, "I can go home by my own self."

"That's all right with me," said Henry crossly.

He knew that now that Ramona went to kindergarten, she was allowed to cross all but the busiest streets alone.

Ramona went her way and Henry went his. When he came to Klickitat Street he found Mrs. Peabody out raking up leaves from her lawn. Ranger, who was lying on the porch, looked suspiciously at Henry, but did not move.

"Why, Harry Higgins!" she exclaimed. "You're all wet."

"Yeah, I know," said Henry sheepishly. He was trying to find a polite way to let Mrs. Peabody know his name was not Harry Higgins. Then his thoughts began to leap. Mrs. Peabody. His paper route. The money for the *Journal.* He had forgotten to get the money from Mrs. Kelly!

Henry's thoughts were in a turmoil as he walked down the street. He could not go back and ask Mrs. Kelly for the money after what had happened. He would just skip the whole thing and pay for the Kellys' papers himself. Nobody would ever know the difference. No, he wouldn't either. He would never save enough for a sleeping bag if he did that. Yes, he would, too. He could never, never bring himself to ring that doorbell again. Yes, he could. No, he could not. That Ramona! She was the cause of all this. A little old kindergartner.

That settled the matter for Henry. He was not going to let a girl in kindergarten keep him from getting the money he had coming to him. Henry turned around and started back toward the Kellys' house.

"Well, Harry, did you forget something?" asked Mrs. Peabody.

"Yes, I did," answered Henry, managing to sound polite. He was so disgusted with Ramona that he felt like snapping at the whole world. First she had told Mrs. Peabody only she could prevent forest fires, and now this. If she ever caused him any more trouble on his paper route he would . . .

he would . . . do something. What he would do he did not know.

Henry marched straight up the steps and rang the Kellys' doorbell.

Lisa looked out of the window smeared with little fingerprints and screamed, "Mommy, it's that boy again!"

When the door opened, Henry was the first to speak. "Mrs. Kelly, I am sorry to bother you again, but I didn't get the money for the paper when I was here before." He was still so disgusted with Ramona he forgot to be embarrassed.

"I thought you would be back." Mrs. Kelly laid down the cellulose sponge in her hand and picked up her purse, which was lying on a chair near the door.

Henry accepted the money and gave Mrs. Kelly a receipt. Whew, he thought, I hope I never have to go through this again. And he decided he had better make sure that he did not. "Uh . . . Mrs.

Kelly," he ventured, "what day would be best for me to collect?"

"The first Saturday of the month," answered Mrs. Kelly. "That is payday."

Henry pulled his route book out of his hip pocket and made a note after the Kellys' name. "Collect 1st Sat." There. That ought to show Mrs. Kelly he could be businesslike. "Thank you," he said, and once more started for home. Now he did not care if he was damp and dirty. He had actually collected from every single one of the forty-three customers on his route. The job was finished until the first of next month and now he could go back to working on the clubhouse.

"Did you get what you went after, Harry?" asked Mrs. Peabody as Henry passed her house for the third time that afternoon.

"I sure did." Henry was now feeling so confident that he was certain someday he would be able to find a way to let Mrs. Peabody know his name was not Harry Higgins. He would even find a way to keep Ramona from causing him trouble on his route. He would find a way to keep her away from the clubhouse, too.

Henry realized that it was now too late for him to do any work on the clubhouse this afternoon. Tomorrow afternoon the first thing he would do was make a sign saying, "No girls allowed."

The only thing wrong with this idea was that Ramona could not read.

CHAPTER FIVE

Ramona and the Clubhouse

WHENEVER it was not raining, Henry and his friends worked hard on the clubhouse. They measured and sawed and nailed, according to Murph's plan. When Henry was delivering his papers he noticed that one of his customers was having his roof covered with asphalt shingles, and he was able to persuade the workmen to give him enough leftover material to shingle the roof of the clubhouse. He bought two big hinges, so they could have a door that would really open and close.

Beezus and Ramona and sometimes Lisa came over almost every day to watch the progress of the building. They stayed until time for the Sheriff Bud program on television, which Ramona never missed.

"I could help," offered Beezus. "I bet I can drive nails."

"No girls allowed," said Murph curtly.

"I could make curtains for the windows," suggested Beezus.

"Who wants curtains?" answered Henry, who would have been willing to let Beezus help, because for a girl she was pretty sensible, but when a boy is working with other boys he sometimes feels he has to act the way they do.

So Beezus sat on the Huggins' back steps and watched, while Ramona amused herself. Ramona never had any trouble keeping herself entertained. She climbed to the top step and began to count, "Ten, nine, eight, seven, six, five, four, three, two, one. *Blast off!*" Then she jumped to the ground.

"I know where I could get an old door mat," suggested Beezus hopefully.

"What's the use of having a clubhouse if you have to wipe your feet like in a regular house?" asked Robert.

It was not possible for Beezus to make a suggestion that would please the boys. "Get lost," said Murph rudely.

"Well, all right for you, smarty!" It was easy to see that Beezus' feelings were hurt. "Mess around with your old boy stuff. See if I care! Come on, Ramona, let's go home. It's almost time for Sheriff Bud."

Ramona finished blasting off and trotted along home with her sister.

Henry was really sorry to see Beezus' feelings hurt, but he did not like to say so in front of the other boys, who were too busy installing the real glass windows to pay any attention to what had just happened.

While the boys worked, Murph began to recite some strange sounds. They were not words, so Henry and Robert had trouble catching exactly what it was he was saying. The syllables, whatever they were, had a catchy sound and rhythm.

"Say that again, Murph." Henry found himself wanting to make the sounds himself.

Once more Murph rattled off the syllables. This time Henry caught a "beep" and a "boom."

"Hey, that sounds keen," said Robert. "Where did you learn that?"

"From my cousin in California," answered Murph. "He learned it from a lifeguard."

"Say it again and slow down," said Henry. "I want to learn it."

Murph laid down his hammer and recited slowly and distinctly.

"Fadatta, fadatta, fadatta,
Beepum, boopum, bah!
Ratta datta boom sh-h
Ahfah deedee bobo."

Henry and Robert laid down their tools, too. "Fadatta . . . fadatta . . . fadatta." They began slowly at first but in a few minutes they had mastered the sounds and could rattle them off as fast as Murph.

"Hey, I have an idea!" Henry was enthusiastic. "We could be a club and use it for our secret password and always say it so fast other kids couldn't learn it."

"Sure," agreed Robert. "All the kids will want to learn it and we won't teach it to them."

"Especially girls." Murph picked up a screw driver and went to work to install the door hinges.

At last the clubhouse was finished. The siding was snug and tight. The hinges worked perfectly, the asphalt shingles were nailed down so securely the roof could not possibly leak. Yes, the boys agreed, it was a good solid house. It was just about as solid as a real house. They thumped the walls appreciatively and stamped their feet on the floor.

And the best part of it was, it was big enough for three boys to sleep in if they didn't move around much, and who could move around in a sleeping bag?

"Yes, sir, solid as the rock of Gibraltar." Murph spoke with pride, for he was the one who had drawn up the plans in the first place.

Then Murph built a shelf and Henry went into the basement and lugged out the stuffed owl which his mother would not let him keep in his room, because she thought it looked as if it had moths. He set the owl on the shelf. It was exactly what the place needed, a really masculine touch.

"Fadatta, fadatta, fadatta," chanted the boys.

"When we all get sleeping bags we can spend the night out here," said Henry.

Robert and Murph, it developed, already had sleeping bags, so Henry dropped the subject. He did not want them sleeping in the clubhouse while he slept in his own bed. Fortunately it was time for him to start his paper route, so there was no more discussion of sleeping in the clubhouse.

Then mysterious things began to happen in the clubhouse. One day after school Henry found the owl's glass eyes turned so that it looked cross-eyed. That's funny, he thought. He straightened the eyes and forgot about them.

But the next day when Henry and Robert entered their clubhouse they were startled to see that the owl, its eyes once again crossed, appeared to be smoking a cigarette. Upon closer examination they found that a small tube of white paper had been fastened to the owl's beak with Scotch tape.

"How do you like that!" Robert ripped off the cigarette in disgust while Henry straightened the eyes once more. "I'll bet old Beezus did this."

That was just what Henry was thinking. He felt

a little disappointed that sensible Beezus would do a thing like this, not that he could really blame her after the way she had been treated. . . .

The boys found a can of paint in Henry's garage and started painting a *No Girls Allowed—This Means You,"* sign, which Robert finished after Henry went to start his paper route.

The next afternoon Henry, Robert, and Murph raced home from school on their bicycles to protect their clubhouse from a possible invasion of Beezus and Ramona. When they opened the door they found the owl's eyes were crossed once more, it was wearing a doll's pink bonnet with a ribbon tied under its chin—if an owl could be said to have a chin—and in its beak it held a crayoned sign that said: *Down with boys!*

"Well, how do you like that!" exclaimed Henry, thinking that Beezus must have come in the morning before school, because they had ridden so fast she could not possibly have reached the clubhouse ahead of them this afternoon.

"The nerve of some people," said Robert. "A doll bonnet on our owl!"

"That's a girl for you." Murph tore down the sign.

"A lock, that's what we need," said Henry.

"A padlock," agreed Murph.

"With a key," said Robert.

Henry dug into his pocket for some of the money he had earned on his route, and the three boys rode off to the hardware store to select a clasp and padlock. When they returned, the owl was holding a sign that said: *Ha ha, you think you are smart.*

Murph screwed the clasp in place, because he was the fastest with tools. While he worked, Henry and Robert decided that because the lock came with only two keys and each member could not have one, they should find two secret hiding places. They talked it over in whispers and after looking around to make sure Beezus was not hiding in the shrubbery, they hid one key under an oilcan in the garage and the other under a flowerpot on the back porch. They vowed always to put the keys back in place, because it would not be fair for any one boy to carry a key when there were not enough keys to go around.

It was with a feeling of a deed well done that the boys snapped shut the padlock when it was time for Henry to start his route. That would keep old Beezus out! She could not possibly get in now. The house was solidly built and the windows taken from the old garage were not the kind that could be opened.

After that the boys had no more trouble. Their next project was painting the house. The front and the north side were to be white, while the back and the south side were to be green. The boys did not have enough paint of one color for the whole house, and anyway, as Murph pointed out, nobody could see all four sides at the same time. Henry painted a little each afternoon before starting his route, and Robert and Murph continued to work after he had gone.

Beezus and Ramona sometimes walked up the driveway to see what was going on. When the boys ignored them, they went away, but they did not go away quietly, because Ramona was always singing some tune or other that she had learned from television. Sometimes it was a song about shampoo, but usually it was a verse about a bread that builds strong bodies eight different ways.

"I guess we fixed her," the boys congratulated one another. "You won't catch her bothering us any more." And when the girls were gone they chanted their magic words:

"Fadatta, fadatta, fadatta,
Beepum, boopum, bah!
Ratta datta boom sh-h
Ahfah deedee bobo."

All for one and one for all. That was Henry, Robert, and Murph.

Then one cold November afternoon Henry came home from school to find that his mother had left a note telling him she had gone downtown and would not be back until six o'clock. She also told him not to eat any pie. Henry used his finger to wipe up some juice that had oozed through the piecrust. *M-m-m.* Blackberry. Then he made himself a peanut-butter sandwich and with Ribsy trotting after him, went outside, where he removed a key from under the flowerpot, unlocked the clubhouse, and carefully returned the key to its hiding place.

Henry stepped inside the clubhouse and patted

the owl's head. Everything was in order. Ribsy curled up in a corner and prepared to go to sleep.

"Hello." It was Ramona's voice.

Henry turned and saw the little girl sitting on the back steps. She was bundled up, because the day was cold and she too was eating a peanut-butter sandwich.

"Oh . . . hello," he said. "Where's Beezus?"

"Home."

"Why didn't she come with you?" Henry felt that Ramona could cause enough trouble when she was with Beezus. He did not want her around without her older sister to look after her.

"Because you are mean to her," answered Ramona.

Henry felt slightly uncomfortable, because there was truth in what Ramona said. Even so, boys had a right to do boy things without girls around, didn't they? And Beezus didn't have to mess up their clubhouse, did she?

He looked at Ramona sitting on the steps chewing her peanut-butter sandwich. "Why don't you go home?" he asked, seeing no reason for being hospitable to Ramona.

"I don't want to," said Ramona, and went on chewing.

Well, as long as she had a sandwich to keep her busy . . . Henry looked around the clubhouse to see how it could be furnished. An orange crate nailed to the wall would make a good cupboard. He measured the space with his hands. Yes, an orange crate would be just the right size.

Henry was aware that the clubhouse had suddenly grown darker. He turned and saw that the door must have blown shut. Just then he heard a *snap* and he had a terrible feeling. He tried the door. It was locked. Locked from the outside and there was only one person who could have done it—Ramona.

Henry looked out of the window and saw

Ramona sitting on the steps, calmly licking her fingers. "You let me out of here!" he yelled.

Ramona stopped licking long enough to answer. "I don't have a key."

This stopped Henry. Of course she did not have a key. Both keys were carefully hidden and he was not going to tell any girl where they were, either. He could get out some way.

Henry threw his shoulder against the door. Nothing happened. It was a good, solid door. He threw his shoulder against the walls. Still nothing happened. They were good solid walls. Henry rubbed his shoulder and decided that Murph had done a good job of planning the clubhouse. Maybe too good.

Next he jumped up and down as hard as he could. The floor was a good solid floor. The whole clubhouse, Henry concluded, was as solidly built as a jail, and right now that was exactly what it was.

Next Henry considered breaking a window. He looked around, but there was not a hammer or a stick of wood he could use. If he slammed his fist through the glass, he would be sure to cut himself, and even if he did break the glass, the windows were divided into four small panes and he had no way of removing the dividing pieces of wood.

Next Henry tried yelling. "Help! Help!" he shouted at the top of his voice. "Help! Help!" Ribsy stood up and barked. Nothing happened. Nothing at all unless you counted the pleased look on Ramona's face. Where was everybody anyway?

"Huh-huh-huh-help," said Ramona, as if she were thinking very hard. Little puffs of vapor came out of her mouth, because the afternoon was so cold. "Help begins with an *h!*" Plainly Ramona was pleased with herself for making this discovery. Her kindergarten teacher was teaching her class the sounds the letters make.

Henry knew that his mother was downtown.

Robert was getting a haircut, Beezus was home, and he did not know where Murph was. Then he caught a glimpse of Mrs. Grumbie, his next-door neighbor looking out of an upstairs window. "Help!" he yelled, pounding on the door. "Let me out!"

Mrs. Grumbie nodded and waved. She was used to boys playing in Henry's back yard.

There was nothing to do, Henry decided, but try to make himself comfortable until his mother came home. He sat down on the floor and leaned against the wall. Ho-hum. It was going to be a long, cold wait. He felt cross and disgusted. That Ramona . . . that pest . . .

Suddenly Henry leaped to his feet. His route! His paper route. He *had* to get out. He could not stay trapped until six o'clock or he wouldn't get his papers delivered in time. And he knew what his father would say about that. Boy!

The only thing to do, Henry decided, was to tell

Ramona where the key was and to get her to unlock the padlock. That would not be so terrible, now that he stopped to think about it. All he would have to do was find another hiding place after Ramona had gone home.

Henry looked out of the window. Ramona was no longer on the steps. Apparently she had lost interest in Henry when he was silent, because now she was skipping down the driveway. He couldn't let her go. She was his only hope.

"Ramona! Wait!" yelled Henry.

Ramona stopped and looked back.

"Come here," called Henry. "I want to tell you something."

This tempted Ramona. She walked back and stood under the clubhouse window, looking up at Henry.

Henry had a feeling that if he was going to get Ramona to do what he wanted he had better make this good. "Uh . . . Ramona, I am going to let you in on a secret. A big secret."

Ramona, who liked secrets, looked interested.

Henry decided to build it up. "A secret that only *boys* know," he added impressively.

"I don't like boys," Ramona informed him. "Boys are mean."

Henry saw that he had better choose his words with more care. At the same time he had to hurry, because it was almost time to start his route. "Only three people in the whole world know the secret." He watched Ramona's reaction. She seemed to be waiting for him to go on.

Henry lowered his voice as much as he could and still make himself heard through the glass. "I am going to tell you where the key to the clubhouse is—"

"Where?" demanded Ramona.

"Wait a minute," said Henry. "First you have to

promise something." He worked hard to look as if there was something mysterious and exciting about the promise he was about to extract, but it was hard work. He was tired of the game and wanted to get out. Now. "If you promise to unlock the padlock, I will tell you where the key is."

Ramona stared stonily at Henry. "I don't want to."

"But *why?*" Henry was desperate.

"I just don't," Ramona informed him.

Oh-h. Henry groaned. Then he was mad, just plain mad. That Ramona! She was going to make him lose his route, and then he would never get his sleeping bag, and his father would be cross with him, and Mr. Capper would find a bigger boy to take the route. . . . Henry banged his fist against the side of the clubhouse. For some reason that made him feel better. He began to stamp his feet and pound his fists and yell. At least, he thought grimly, this was keeping Ramona interested. And he couldn't let her get away. She was his only hope . . . almost, it seemed, his only contact with civilization. It occurred to him that it must be almost time for the Sheriff Bud program on television, and Ramona never missed Sheriff Bud.

It seemed silly to yell "help!" and "let me out!" when nobody was going to help him or let him out. Henry tried a Tarzan yell. Ramona sat down on the back steps and propped her chin up on her fist.

"Open Sesame!" yelled Henry, just in case it might work. The door remained shut.

Then in desperation Henry tried the club yell, hoping that somehow it would work like a magic spell.

"Fadatta, fadatta, fadatta,
Beepum, boopum, bah!
Ratta datta boom sh-h
Ahfah deedee bobo!"

To his surprise it did work like a magic spell. Ramona got up and came over to the clubhouse window. "Say that again, Henry," she begged.

This time it was Henry's turn to say no. To do so gave him great satisfaction.

"Please, Henry."

Henry saw that he had a bargaining point. A girl who would sing television commercials would naturally like something that sounded really good. "I'll say it again if you get the key and unlock the padlock first."

Ramona thought it over. "Puh-puh-puh-padlock begins with a *p!*" she said triumphantly.

Henry groaned. "I *know* padlock begins with a *p*," he said. "Now will you get the key?" Then he added hastily. "Key begins with a *k*."

"We haven't had *k* yet at school." Ramona seemed suddenly agreeable. "Where is the key?" she asked.

Feeling like a traitor to Robert and Murph,

Henry revealed the secret. "Under the flowerpot on the back porch."

Ramona found the key and Henry could hear her fumbling as she inserted it in the padlock. "Say it," she ordered.

Henry rattled off the club's secret words. "Now unlock it," he begged, and outside he could hear Ramona struggling with the padlock.

"I can't," she said. "I can't make the key turn."

Henry pressed his nose against the window. "Look," he said, "go get Beezus. If you do, I'll teach you both to say fadatta, fadatta, fadatta. And . . . tell her I'm sorry."

I am a traitor, thought Henry, a one-hundred-per-cent traitor. But what else could he do? He had to get his papers delivered somehow. Then he began to worry about Ramona. Maybe she would forget to tell Beezus. Maybe she would remember Sheriff Bud, turn on the television set, and forget all about him.

There was nothing Henry could do but wait. Actually he did not wait very long, but it seemed that way. It seemed to him that he waited and waited and waited. The clubhouse felt colder and damper and more like a dungeon every minute.

At last Henry heard footsteps coming up the driveway. Beezus had come to his rescue—he hoped. Beezus was alone, and Henry guessed that Ramona had stayed home to watch television. "Hi, Beezus," he called through the window. "It's sure nice of you to come and let me out . . . after the way I have . . . uh . . . acted." The last words Henry found difficult to speak, but he felt better when he had said them.

Beezus looked as if she had not made up her mind to let Henry out. "I didn't say I was going to let you out," she reminded him. "You don't want girls around, you know."

Henry had no answer for this. "Aw, come on, Beezus," he pleaded. "I've got to start my route."

Beezus thought it over. "All right, I'll let you out, but only because I know you have to start your route," she agreed, like the sensible girl she was. "But first teach me the secret words."

Henry knew when he was licked. "Oh, all right, if that's the way you feel about it. Fadatta . . . fadatta . . . fadatta."

"Fadatta . . . fadatta . . . fadatta," Beezus repeated gravely.

"Beepum, boopum, bah."

"Beepum, boopum, bah." Fortunately Beezus learned quickly and soon mastered the secret words. She was a girl who kept her part of the bargain. She unlocked the padlock and slipped it out of the clasp. "There," she said.

"Thanks, Beezus," said Henry, as he stepped out to fresh air and freedom. He picked up his bicycle. He had no time to talk if he was going to get his papers folded and delivered.

Beezus did not seem to mind that Henry was in

such a hurry. "Fadatta, fadatta, fadatta," she chanted. "Good-by, Henry. I'm going home to teach the secret words to Ramona like I promised."

Henry threw his leg over his bicycle and pedaled down the driveway. Now the secret words would be all over the neighborhood. Robert and Murph would not like it, but Henry hoped that since they knew Ramona they would understand and not mind too much.

That Ramona! thought Henry. Always causing him trouble on his route. He would have to do something about her, but what anybody could do about Ramona, he did not know. All he knew was that if he was going to keep his paper route and his clubhouse he had better do something, and do it soon.

CHAPTER SIX

Henry Writes a Letter

NATURALLY as soon as Ramona learned the secret words, she recited them every chance she got and soon they were all over the neighborhood. They were all over Glenwood School, too. Everywhere Henry went he heard fadattas and beepum, boo-pum, bahs. He began to wish he had never heard the silly thing. Quite a few mothers felt this way, too, and asked their children *please* to stop saying that—that *thing*. But the whole school went right on saying fadatta, fadatta, fadatta.

And all because of Ramona. Yes, Henry decided, something was going to have to be done about Ramona, but what he did not know.

"Say, Mom," Henry said one evening, "how can I keep Ramona from being such an awful pest all the time?"

"Just don't pay any attention to her," answered Mrs. Huggins.

"But Mom," protested Henry. "You don't know Ramona."

Mrs. Huggins laughed. "Yes, I do. She is just a lively little girl who gets into mischief sometimes. Ignore her, and she will stop bothering you. She only wants attention."

Henry could not help feeling that his mother did not understand the situation. He had ignored Ramona. That was the whole trouble. He was not paying any attention to her so he had found himself locked in the clubhouse. This was not a little mischief. It was a terrible thing for her to do.

"Surely you are smarter than a five-year-old," remarked Mr. Huggins jokingly.

Henry did not have an answer for his father, who, after all, was safe in his office all day and did not know what a nuisance Ramona could be.

Next Henry consulted Beezus. "Ramona sure causes me a lot of trouble on my route," he remarked one afternoon. "Isn't there some way to get her to stop pestering me?"

Beezus sighed. "I know. I've told Mother, and Mother has told her to behave herself, but you know how Ramona is. She never listens."

"I know," Henry said gloomily. Ramona was a real problem. When Mrs. Quimby persuaded her to stop doing one annoying thing, Ramona promptly thought up something entirely new but equally annoying. If only Henry could find a way to stay ahead of Ramona. . . .

One afternoon Henry arrived at Mr. Capper's garage in plenty of time to fold his papers. He counted his stack of forty-three *Journals* and as long as he was early, he took time to glance through the paper. He looked at the headlines and read the comic section. Then a picture of a smiling lady caught his eye. It was the lady who gave people advice when they wrote to her about their problems.

Because he had a problem, Henry paused to read her column. A girl who signed her letter, "Flat Broke" said that her father did not give her a big enough allowance. Her father did not understand that she needed more money for school lunches, bus fare, and other things. What should she do about it? The smiling lady told her to talk it over with her father and explain to him exactly what her expenses were. The smiling lady was sure he would understand.

Henry thought this over. Maybe he should write

to the lady about Ramona. He could write, I have a problem. A girl in my neighborhood has a little sister who pesters me on my paper route. How can I get her to stop? Then he could sign the letter Disgusted.

Henry tried to think how the lady would answer his letter. Dear Disgusted, she would say, but what would she say next? Probably she would tell him to talk his problem over with Ramona's mother and everything would be all right. Oh no, it wouldn't, thought Henry, just as if he had really read an answer to a letter he had really written. Ramona's mother knew all about his problem and had not been able to solve it. As Beezus said, Ramona never listened very much.

Henry began to fold his papers. There must be somebody Ramona would listen to. And then a picture in an advertisement gave Henry an idea. Santa Claus! Ramona might listen to Santa Claus. Henry grinned to himself. He would really fix

Ramona if he waited until Christmas Eve and climbed up on the Quimbys' roof and yelled down the chimney in a deep bass voice, Ho-ho-ho, Ramona Geraldine Quimby, you stop pestering Henry Huggins on his paper route or I won't leave you any presents. Ho-ho-ho.

"Ho-ho-ho," said Henry out loud, to see how much like Santa Claus he could sound.

Just then Mr. Capper came out of the back door. "Who do you think you are? Santa Claus?" he asked.

"No, sir." Embarrassed, Henry went on folding papers.

Still, Henry was pleased with this picture of himself ho-ho-hoing down the chimney at Ramona, but unfortunately there was just one thing wrong with it. Boys were not allowed to go climbing around on their neighbors' roofs on Christmas Eve or any other time. And anyway, Ramona

might not even listen to Santa Claus. Henry would not be at all surprised.

Henry was zigzagging down the street on his bicycle, throwing papers to the right and to the left, when he saw Beezus and Ramona hurrying along the sidewalk. Ramona was wearing a mustache cut from brown paper and stuck to her upper lip with Scotch tape. Henry recognized this as another attempt to copy one of Sheriff Bud's disguises.

"Hi, Beezus," he said.

Ramona pulled at Beezus' hand. "Come on," she said. "Come on, or we'll be late."

"I can't understand it," remarked Beezus. "She can't even tell time, but she always knows when it's time for the Sheriff Bud program."

"Like Ribsy," said Henry. "He can't tell time either, but he always knows when it's time to meet me after school." He pedaled on down the street, when suddenly a thought struck him. *Sheriff Bud.* If there was anyone Ramona would listen to, it was Sheriff Bud.

Henry was so excited by this inspiration that he threw a paper on the wrong porch and had to go back to get it. Of course she would listen to Sheriff Bud, but how could Henry get Sheriff Bud to tell Ramona to stop pestering him on his paper route? Write him a letter, that's what he would do. Sheriff Bud was always waving around handfuls of letters and wishing listeners happy birthdays and hoping they would get over the measles or something. He was always pretending he could see people in the television audience, too. Henry had never heard him tell a listener to stop pestering someone, but there was no reason why he couldn't. It would be worth trying anyway.

As soon as Henry finished his route he went home and turned on the television set. There was Sheriff Bud in his ten-gallon hat. This time he was wearing a false nose. He held a microphone in one hand, and between commercials was interviewing a row of children who had microphones hung around their necks. All the children said hello to many, many friends out in television land. Henry thought it was a silly program, although he still sometimes watched the cartoons that were shown between the endless commercials.

Ordinarily when Henry wrote a letter he used the typewriter, because it was more fun than pen and ink, but today he was in too much of a hurry to hunt around and poke all those keys. He found a piece of paper and a pen, and after his address and the date, began, "Dear Sherrif." That looked peculiar so he added another *f*. "Dear Sherriff" still looked peculiar so he consulted the dictionary.

Then Henry tore up his letter and started over. "Dear Sheriff Bud," he wrote in his best handwriting. "I need your help. There is this girl who pesters me on my paper route. She always watches your program so could you please tell her to stop pestering me? Her name is Ramona Geraldine Quimby. Thank you." Then he signed his name, addressed an envelope to Sheriff Bud in care of the television station, found a stamp, and went out to mail the letter.

As soon as the mailbox clanked shut, Henry knew his scheme would not work. Sheriff Bud received thousands of letters every week. He was always talking about the thousands of letters he received. He waved great handfuls of them around. Why would he pay any attention to one letter and a pretty smudgy one, at that?

But doubtful as he was, Henry somehow hung

on to a faint hope that Sheriff Bud might really read his letter and help him out. The letter would be delivered the next day but he might not have time to read it before the program went on the air. Maybe the day after . . .

Two days later Henry rang the Quimbys' doorbell about the time the Sheriff Bud program was starting. "Hello, Beezus," he said, when his friend opened the door. "I was wondering—how about a game of checkers before I start my route?"

Beezus looked surprised. She and Henry used to play checkers often, but since he had become a paper carrier and spent so much time working on the clubhouse, he had not found time to play with her. "Why . . . yes, come on in."

As Henry had expected, Ramona was sitting on a hassock in the living room watching Sheriff Bud, who today was wearing sideburns. While Beezus got out the checker set, Henry watched the program.

"And I want all you little folks out in T.V. land to do something for old Sheriff Bud," the Sheriff was saying. "I want you to tell Mother right now, *right this very minute,* to put Crispy Potato Chips, the potato chips positively guaranteed never to bend, on her shopping list. Yes, sirree, this *very minute.*" His smile filled the whole screen.

"Mother!" called Ramona. "Sheriff Bud says—"

"I don't care what Sheriff Bud says," answered Mrs. Quimby from the kitchen. She sounded very cross. "I can make out my grocery list without that man's help."

Beezus set up the checker board on the coffee table and, kneeling, she and Henry began to play. For once Ramona did not bother them, but Henry found it difficult to think about the game and try to follow Sheriff Bud at the same time. They both stopped playing whenever a cartoon came on, but Beezus had no trouble beating him twice in succession.

Once when the sheriff waved a sheaf of letters Henry's hopes rose, but Sheriff Bud only wished a lot of people happy birthday and told how many people had written in to say they liked Nutsies, the candy bar chockfull of energy. Henry wished he had said in his letter that both he and Ramona ate Nutsies all the time. And Crispy Potato Chips, too.

By the time the program had ended Beezus had defeated Henry a third time. Naturally Henry could not let this record stand. "I bet I can beat you tomorrow," he volunteered.

"I bet you can't," said Beezus, "but you can come over and try."

Henry left, and by working fast delivered all his papers on time. The next afternoon he once more presented himself at the Quimbys' front door, this time to show Beezus he really could beat her at checkers. He would forget all about Sheriff Bud. It had been silly of him to think his letter would be read out of all the thousands the television station received. Beezus had the checkers waiting on the coffee table and as usual Ramona was sitting on the hassock watching Sheriff Bud, who was wearing a pair of large false ears. His voice filled the living room.

"Ramona, turn that program down!" called Mrs. Quimby from the kitchen.

Ramona did not budge.

This time Henry was determined to ignore even the cartoons. Beezus made the first move with a red checker and Henry moved his black checker. Beezus jumped him, he jumped her, and the game was on.

"And now, kiddies out there in T.V. land, if Mother doesn't have a cupboard full of—" Sheriff Bud was saying.

Mrs. Quimby appeared in the living room. "Ramona, turn that thing off. I am sick and tired of listening to that man tell me what to buy."

"No!" screamed Ramona. "No! I don't want to turn it off."

"Then turn it *down*," said Mrs. Quimby, and went back into the kitchen. This time Ramona lowered the sound of the television set slightly.

"Your move," Beezus reminded Henry.

Henry studied the board. If he moved there, Beezus could jump him. If he moved there, he could jump her if she moved her man in the right direction.

"And now for today's mail," announced Sheriff Bud.

Henry could not help glancing at the television screen. Sheriff Bud was holding the usual handful of letters, but this time he was pointing straight ahead at someone in the television audience. "Ramona Geraldine Quimby, I see you out there," he said. "I see you out in T.V. land."

Henry and Beezus dropped their checkers. Mrs. Quimby stepped out of the kitchen. Ramona clasped her hands together and her eyes grew round. "He sees me," she said in awe.

"Ramona Geraldine Quimby," said Sheriff Bud, "I want you to do something that will make old Sheriff Bud very, very happy."

"Whatever it is, I'm not going to buy it." Mrs. Quimby sounded indignant.

Ramona leaned forward, her eyes wide, her mouth open.

Henry's eyes were just about as wide and his mouth was open, too.

Sheriff Bud sounded as if he and Ramona were alone. "Ramona, it will make old Sheriff Bud very, very happy if you stop pestering"—he stopped

and squinted at a letter in his hand—"Henry Huggins on his paper route. Do you promise?"

"Yes." Ramona barely whispered.

"Good," said Sheriff Bud. "We've got to get those papers delivered. If you stop pestering Henry on his route, you will make me just about as happy as it would if you told Mother you wanted Crispy Potato Chips for lunch every day. And now—"

But no one was listening to the television set.

"Henry!" shrieked Beezus. "Did you hear that?"

"I sure did." Henry was feeling a little awed himself. It had seemed as if Sheriff Bud really could see Ramona. He could not, of course, but . . .

"Honestly!" Mrs. Quimby snapped off the television set. "That man will do anything to squeeze in more commercials. Crispy Potato Chips! Really!"

Only Ramona was silent. She did not even object to her mother's turning off the television set.

She turned to Henry with her eyes wide with awe. "Do you really know Sheriff Bud?" she asked.

"Well . . . I guess you might say he is a friend of mine," said Henry and added, to himself, Now.

Then Mrs. Quimby spoke to her youngest daughter. "Ramona, have you been pestering Henry on his paper route again?"

Ramona looked as if she were about to cry. "I—I won't do it any more," she said.

"That's a good girl," said Mrs. Quimby. "Delivering papers is an important job and you mustn't get in Henry's way."

"I bet I know how Sheriff Bud knew about it," said Beezus with a smile. "Your move, Henry."

Henry grinned as he advanced his checker. Beezus promptly jumped and captured two of his men. Oh, well, what did he care? It was only a game. His paper route was real.

Henry grimaced at Ramona who smiled back almost shyly. Henry moved another checker, which Beezus captured. He did not care. His paper route was safe from Ramona. If she pestered him again, all he had to do was to say, "Remember Sheriff Bud," and his troubles would be over. It was as easy as that. He had finally hit upon a good idea that had nothing wrong with it. Not one single thing.

"I won!" Beezus was triumphant.

"I'll beat you in the next game," said Henry, and this time he was sure he would.

CHAPTER SEVEN

Henry's Little Shadow

AFTERWARDS Henry realized that he should have known something would go wrong with his plan to keep Ramona from pestering him. Now, because he was a friend of Sheriff Bud, Henry had become such a hero to Ramona that she wanted to follow him wherever he went. Next, Mrs. Quimby said that she was disgusted with the Sheriff Bud program and Ramona was not to watch it any more. Not ever. This left Ramona plenty of time for tagging after Henry.

The worst part of it was there was nothing Henry could do about Ramona's tagging along, because she behaved herself. She stood quietly on Mr. Capper's driveway while Henry folded his papers. Henry began to wish she would pester him so he could yell at her to go away. Fortunately, none of the other paper carriers thought much about her, because many small children in the neighborhood admired the big boys who delivered the papers. Henry was always glad to spring on his bicycle and ride away from her. If he had delivered his papers on foot she would have tagged after him.

Then one day at school Beezus said, "Henry, I don't think you are going to like what Ramona is going to get for Christmas."

"What is she getting?" asked Henry.

Beezus looked worried. "I'm not supposed to tell. I just thought I better warn you is all."

Henry did not know what to make of this message. He did not see how a doll or whatever it was that a girl in kindergarten was going to get for Christmas could bother him. As for himself, he hoped he would get a sleeping bag, because he had not saved his paper-route money as fast as he had expected. He had spent quite a bit on nails and a padlock for the clubhouse, and when he counted the money he had collected for his paper route he found he was short a couple of dollars and realized he must have made some mistakes in giving change. This cut into his profits, and after he had done his Christmas shopping he was still several dollars short of a sleeping bag.

Henry was not disappointed on Christmas morning when he opened a big package and found, not a sleeping bag, but a microscope. He could have a lot of fun with a microscope. It was so cold his mother would not let him sleep outdoors anyway, and next month he would have enough money to buy the sleeping bag.

It was not until Christmas afternoon, when Henry was folding his papers, that Henry found out what Beezus meant. He looked up and saw Ramona standing there on the driveway in her snow suit. Henry dropped the paper he was folding when he saw that over her shoulders she was wearing a cloth bag, a small copy of the one *Journal* carriers wore. It even had *READ THE*

JOURNAL embroidered on it in red yarn. Embroidered! It was terrible. In each half of her bag Ramona carried some old rolled-up newspapers. She also carried a battered Teddy bear in the front half. She was smiling proudly.

Naturally the other carriers practically laughed themselves sick at the sight of Henry's admirer. Red with embarrassment, Henry tried to pretend he did not see Ramona. He bent over and folded papers as fast as he could, so he could get out of there.

"Henry, see what Santa Claus brought me," said Ramona, ignoring the laughter. "Now I can be a paper boy like you."

The other boys whooped.

"Why don't you go home?" Henry asked crossly.

"I want to watch," said Ramona politely.

Henry could see that in spite of the boys' laughter Ramona was proud of her very own *Journal* bag, and there was nothing he could do about it, because she had kept her promise to Sheriff Bud and was being good. Henry could see that another of his good ideas had turned out wrong. Even when Ramona was good she was a problem.

Then Beezus, wearing a brand-new Christmas car coat with a hood, came hurrying up the driveway. "Come on home, Ramona," she said, then turned to Henry. "I tried to warn you. A *Journal* bag was the only thing she wanted for Christmas and so Mother had to make her one. She had a terrible time. She couldn't find a pattern."

Henry slung his bag of *Journals* over his shoulders. "Thanks anyway," he said ruefully, as he threw his leg over his bicycle and rode away from Ramona and the laughter of the other boys.

The next morning, when Henry woke up, he discovered that snow was beginning to fall, a few light flakes at first and then more and larger flakes. What luck! Snow during Christmas vacation. He looked out of his bedroom window and saw that there was already an inch of snow on the roof of the clubhouse. After breakfast Henry dragged his Flexible Flyer out of the basement to have it ready, in case there was enough snow for coasting.

All morning snow fell. By noon it was easy to roll up a snow man. The police blocked off a hill not far from Henry's house and all the boys and girls went coasting. Henry slid so much and got into so many snow fights he had to go home and put his clothes through his mother's clothes dryer before he could go out again.

Cars that did not have snow tires slipped on the icy pavement and skidded into the curbs. Some people who were fortunate enough to have their chains with them thump-thumped down the streets as the snow packed down into ice. By three o'clock Mr. Huggins came driving slowly up the street and skidded gently into a drift at the foot of the driveway. He said the stores downtown were closed and many people could not get across the bridges, because the streets were blocked by skidding cars. Mrs. Huggins looked into the refrigerator and the cupboards to see how much food she had on hand, because she could not go to market and there was no telling when the milkman could get through.

The whole city was in a wonderful state of confusion, and Henry enjoyed every minute of it. He hoped it would be days, even weeks, before the snow thawed. Then the mailman, a muffler tied over his ears and his hat on top of that, came puffing up the steps hours late. The sight of him reminded Henry that he too had work to do, and it was not going to be easy in this weather. Snow or no snow, the *Journal* had to be delivered.

Henry dried his woolen gloves in the dryer for the third time that day before he started out, this time on foot. At Mr. Capper's garage he had a long cold wait before the truck that brought the papers was able to get through. FOOT OF SNOW BLANKETS CITY was the headline that day.

In spite of the cold Ramona also waited in her snow suit with her little *Journal* bag over her shoulders. She kept busy by making a snowman on the driveway. "Fadatta, fadatta, fadatta," she said to herself as she worked. When the snowman was finished she tried her *Journal* bag on it. Henry hoped she would leave it there but she did not. She put it over her own shoulders again.

When Henry had managed to fold his papers with fingers numbed by the cold, he discovered that this time Ramona could tag after him, because he had to cover his route on foot. And follow him through the snow she did, about ten feet behind him, even though walking was not easy. In some places the snow had drifted, in others it was packed down into ice. Henry walked as fast as he could, but Ramona struggled along after him.

A man who was trying to shovel snow in front of his house grinned at Henry and said, "I see you have a little shadow."

Henry was mighty glad to see Beezus clumping through the snow in her boots. "Come on home, Ramona," she coaxed. "It's getting colder."

"No," said Ramona. "I want to go with Henry." She trudged along in her boots and there was nothing for Beezus to do but follow along and keep an eye on her.

Henry threw the first paper, which landed with a *plop* in the snow that had drifted on his customer's front steps. Softly a few flakes of snow fell on the paper. This isn't going to work, thought Henry. The papers would get buried on this side of the street, where the snow was drifting. Nobody would be able to find them. He struggled up the front walk, his heavy *Journal* bag banging against his legs, and picked the paper out of the drift. Then he rang the doorbell and handed the paper to his customer, who thanked him and said with a smile, "I see you have a little shadow."

"Yeah," said Henry, without enthusiasm.

Henry soon saw that it was too much work to wade through drifts with his *Journal* bag bumping against his legs. "Beezus, do me a favor, will you?" he asked. "Go get my sled for me."

"It will take quite a while if I have to take Ramona with me," said Beezus. "I could go faster without her."

Henry realized this was true. Ramona's legs were short and the snow was almost to the top of her boots. He did need that sled, though. "O.K., she can tag along with me," he said, knowing she would, whether he wanted her to or not.

Silently Ramona floundered along after him, and Henry grudgingly admitted to himself that she was not pestering him. She had a perfect right to be on the sidewalk, didn't she? If only she were not wearing that ridiculous *Journal* bag. And if only everyone he met would not say, "I see you have a little shadow."

Once Ramona said companionably, "There is an easy house number. One zero zero one." She was proud of her new ability to read numbers. Henry did not answer her.

It was not long until Beezus came, dragging Henry's sled behind her. He was mighty glad to lift the papers from his shoulders and set them on the sled.

"Come on, Ramona," coaxed Beezus. "You can be a paper boy some other day."

"No, I can't," said Ramona, in a small voice. "Henry always rides his bicycle, and I can't keep up with him." So on they trudged.

The next house on the snowdrift side of the street was the house of Mrs. Peabody. Henry took a paper from his sled, waded up to the front door and rang the doorbell.

"Why, it's Harry Higgins!" exclaimed Mrs. Peabody, opening the door just a crack so the cold would not come in. "My, but you are a thoughtful boy to bring the paper right to the front door!"

"His name isn't Harry Higgins!" Ramona shouted. "His name is Henry Huggins!"

Mrs. Peabody looked startled and opened the door a bit wider. "Is it really?" she asked Henry.

"Well . . . yes," admitted Henry, "but that's all right." Just the same he was grateful to Ramona for straightening Mrs. Peabody out. He felt almost kindly toward the little girl in spite of that terrible *Journal* bag.

"My, I am sorry," said Mrs. Peabody. "To think that I have been calling you Harry Higgins all this time when your name is really Henry Huggins. I don't see how I could have made such a mistake."

"Aw, I knew who you meant." Henry was embarrassed.

Ramona began to cry.

"Come on, let's go home," said Beezus impatiently.

Ramona cried harder. "I—I'm too t-tired," she sobbed.

"Why, the poor little thing," said Mrs. Peabody. "She's all worn out. If I could get my car out of the garage I would drive her home myself."

Henry looked at Ramona, standing there sobbing in the snow. Her face was red with cold and blotched with tears. With her boots buried in snow she looked even smaller than she really was. She rubbed her eyes with her cold, soggy mitten, and sniffed pitifully.

Henry's feelings were all mixed up. He remembered how she had locked him in the clubhouse and what a pest she had been. At the same time he was grateful to her, because she had told Mrs. Peabody his real name. Doggone it, thought Henry. Doggone it all anyway. Why did this have to go and happen? He felt sorry for Ramona—actually felt sorry for her. This was really the last straw. He did not want to feel sorry for Ramona in that stupid old *Journal* bag of hers. He tried hard not to feel sorry for her but he could not help himself.

"Come on, Ramona," he said, even though he didn't want to. "Get on the sled and I'll pull you home."

"I'll help," said Beezus gratefully. She lifted her little sister onto the sled in front of Henry's papers. "Now hang on."

Henry and Beezus took the rope and began to pull the sled. By this time the streets were almost empty of cars, and they could run, slipping and sliding, on the snow that had been packed down into ice.

Ramona stopped crying. "Mush!" she yelled between sniffs. "Mush!"

"Aw, keep quiet," said Henry rudely. He was in no mood to play sled dog for Ramona. He did not feel *that* sorry for her.

"Oh, thank you, Henry," said Beezus, when they had deposited Ramona on her front steps. "I don't know how I would ever have got her home without your help."

"That's O.K.," said Henry gruffly, and retraced his steps to start his route once more. And all because of Ramona. It seemed to Henry that he had never had a worse time delivering papers, not even when there was an extra-thick Sunday edition. Half his papers had to be delivered to the door or at least stuffed into the mailbox. He was too warm inside his car coat, but an icy wind began to blow through his trousers, chilling his legs. His boots were heavy and his gloves were wet again. He was tired, cross, and hungry. By the time Henry had delivered his last paper and dragged his sled home again, it was dark and snow was falling through patches of light cast by the street lamps.

"Henry, I was beginning to worry about you," said Mrs. Huggins, when he had stamped the snow off his boots and entered the kitchen.

"It takes longer to deliver papers in the snow," Mr. Huggins pointed out.

"It sure does, Dad," agreed Henry. "It sure does." And he thought, especially when someone like Ramona lives on the route.

The next day the snow had stopped and the sun shone on a sparkling world. The city began to recover. Snowplows cleared the main streets and by late afternoon most of Henry's neighbors had shoveled their walks. Henry was rested but so was Ramona. As soon as he started his paper route, there she was again wearing her little *Journal* bag. Henry wished all the snow was cleared away, so he could ride his bicycle again. Ramona, still very good, tagged along, and all the people who were now shoveling their driveways stopped working and smiled and said, "I see you have a little shadow." There was nothing Henry could do about it. A line of the poem he had once had to speak in school kept running through his head.

> "I have a little shadow that goes in and out with
> me,
> And what can be the use of him is more than
> I can see."

Boy, whoever wrote that poem knew what he was talking about!

The third day just enough snow had fallen to freeze on the cleared sidewalks and make them too slippery for Henry to ride his bicycle. Because delivering papers was still difficult Henry and the other boys gathered early to fold and count the papers. Henry was almost ready to start his route when Mr. Capper came around to check on the boys. He grinned at Henry. "Well, Henry," he said, "I see you got your name in the paper."

"Who, me?" asked Henry in surprise.

"Yes, Henry Huggins," said Mr. Capper, opening a paper. "Right here on the editorial page."

Henry could not understand what Mr. Capper was talking about. What would his name be doing on the editorial page or any place else in the paper? It must be some other Henry Huggins.

Mr. Capper began to read. "Dear Editor."

Henry understood that much. Someone had written a letter to the newspaper.

"Dear Editor," Mr. Capper read. "I wish to call attention to the fine work a boy named Henry Huggins is doing delivering the *Journal* in our neighborhood."

"Hey, that's me!" exclaimed Henry.

"I told you," said Mr. Capper, and continued reading for all the boys to hear. "Henry is always prompt and courteous, but it was yesterday during the heavy snow that I was particularly impressed with his work. Delivering papers that day was not easy, but Henry went out of his way to ring my doorbell and hand me my paper so that it would not get buried in a snowdrift. Not only that, he took time out from his route to give a little girl who was cold and tired a ride home on his sled. The *Journal* should be proud of this fine young citizen. Sincerely yours, Bessie Peabody."

At first Henry was speechless and then he felt as if he was suddenly growing about four inches taller.

All the other carriers looked at Henry with respect.

"Boy, I wish somebody would write a letter like that about me!" said Scooter.

"I've been delivering papers three years and nobody ever wrote a letter about me," said Joe.

"Me neither," said all the other boys.

"And Henry is our youngest carrier," Mr. Capper reminded them. He gave Henry a friendly slap on the shoulder. "Keep up the good work, Henry. I am proud of you."

Henry felt himself grow another inch. Mr. Capper was proud of him! He had said so in front of all the other boys.

On his way down the driveway Henry passed Ramona with her little *Journal* bag over her shoulders. She slipped on an icy spot and sat down hard. Before she could start to howl Henry boosted her to her feet, because he suddenly realized that if it weren't for Ramona, Mrs. Peabody would have written a letter to the *Journal* praising Harry Higgins, and Mr. Capper would have thought it was about a carrier in some other neighborhood.

Henry knew he had had a very close call. "Be

careful and don't fall again," he cautioned Ramona. "You might get hurt." Then he started delivering papers, with Ramona following ten feet behind him. Today this did not bother him. Mr. Capper was proud of him, so he did not care who tagged after him. Besides, he was too busy thinking what his father would say when he read Mrs. Peabody's letter in his evening paper.

Henry decided not to say anything to his father. He would let him discover the letter for himself. His father would be reading along and all of a sudden he would see Henry's name in the paper. He would probably be so surprised he would just about jump out of his chair. . . .

That evening it seemed to Henry that his father never would get around to reading the paper. First he dawdled over his dessert and asked for a second cup of coffee.

"Why are you so restless tonight?" Mr. Huggins asked Henry.

"Me? I'm not restless," said Henry, wishing his father would hurry up and drink that coffee.

"I'll carry your dishes into the kitchen, Dad," Henry offered.

Mr. Huggins looked surprised. He got up from the table and remarked, "Maybe I'll build a fire in the fireplace, it's such a cold night."

"That's funny, Dad," said Henry. "I was just thinking it was awfully warm in here."

Mr. Huggins turned on the television set.

That was too much for Henry. He couldn't wait any longer. "Say, Dad, did you read tonight's paper?" he asked.

"I glanced at the headlines. Why?"

"Well—I just wondered if you happened to read the editorial page," said Henry.

"Not yet." Mr. Huggins looked curiously at his son. "Why are you so interested?"

"I got my name in the paper." Henry could not keep the pride out of his voice.

"On the editorial page?" Mr. Huggins sounded disbelieving as he reached for the evening paper. He folded it back to the editorial page.

"There." Henry pointed at the letter.

"What is it?" asked Mrs. Huggins, coming in from the kitchen. She leaned over her husband's shoulder to read. "Why, Henry!" she exclaimed. "Wasn't that a nice thing for Mrs. Peabody to do for you!"

"Henry, I am proud of you!" said Mr. Huggins. "I don't care how much snow there is. I'm going right out and buy half a dozen papers so we can send copies of this to your relatives."

"Gee, thanks, Dad," said Henry modestly. He had waited a long time to hear his father say he was proud of him.

"I'll admit that when you took on the route and then got mixed up in building a clubhouse, I didn't think you could handle it, but you've done a good job," said Mr. Huggins.

Henry was pleased and at the same time a little embarrassed by this praise from his father.

Mr. Huggins went to the hall closet and put on his overcoat and hat. "By the way," he remarked, "how much more money do you need for that sleeping bag?"

"About five dollars," Henry admitted.

Mr. Huggins took out his wallet, opened it and handed Henry a five-dollar bill. "There you are. Tomorrow you go to the sporting-goods store and buy that sleeping bag."

"Thanks, Dad." Henry accepted the bill. "You mean I can sleep out in the clubhouse when there is snow?"

Mrs. Huggins spoke up. "You may not. Do you think I want you catching your death of cold?"

"But the sleeping bag is filled with down," Henry pointed out. "It's nice and warm."

"I don't care," said Mrs. Huggins. "You can't sleep out until we have some warm dry weather."

"O.K., Mom." Henry was agreeable, because he had not really expected his mother to let him sleep outdoors in the snow. He would have the sleeping bag and that was what counted. That, and knowing his father and Mr. Capper were proud of him and realized he could handle a paper route.

"Coming with me, Henry?" asked Mr. Huggins.

"Sure, Dad." Henry pulled his coat out of the closet. Good old Mrs. Peabody, he thought to himself as he put on his cap and pulled the ear flaps down over his ears. I knew she would be the best customer on my route. He picked up the paper to admire his name in print once more, and as he looked at it he could not help thinking, Good old Ramona.

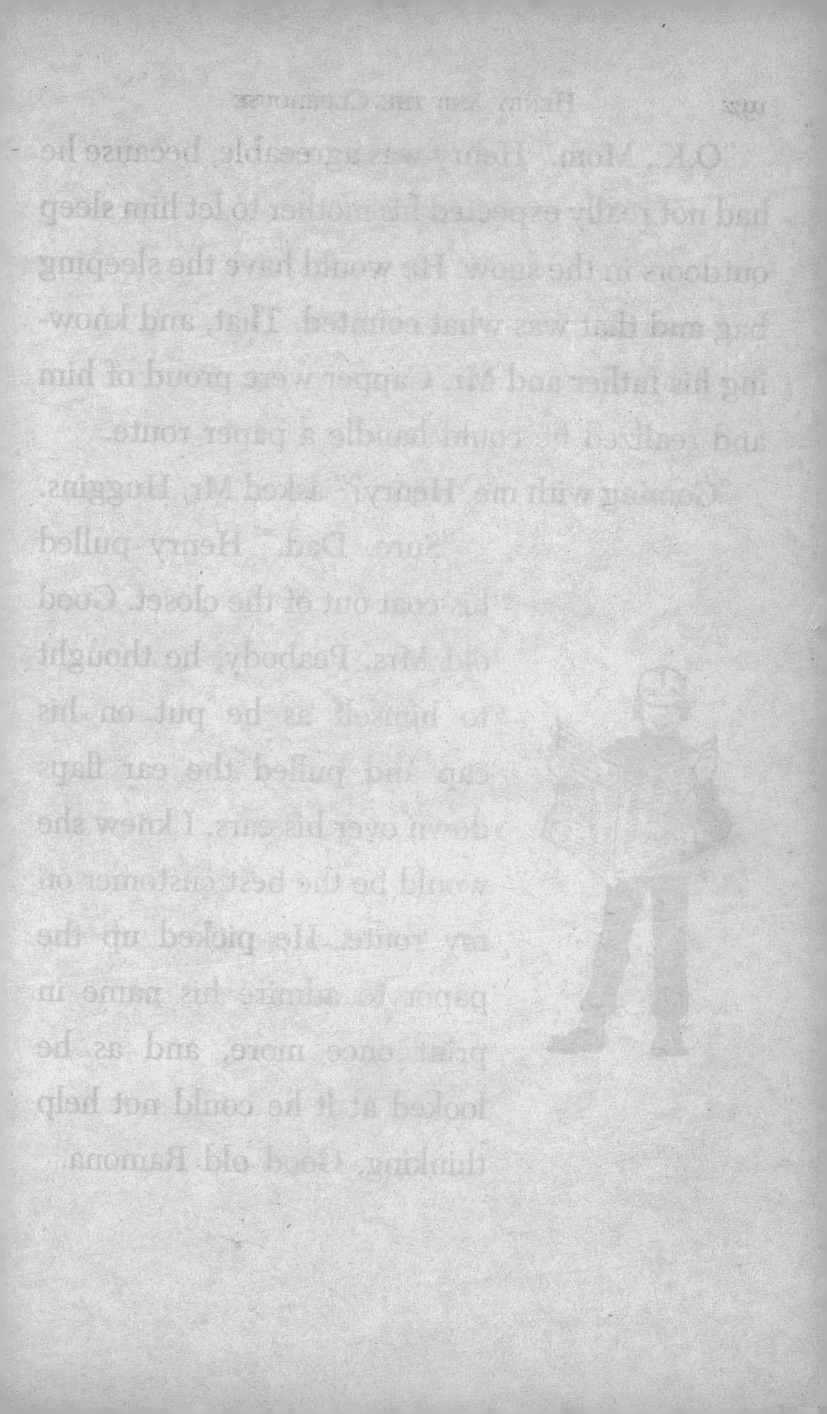

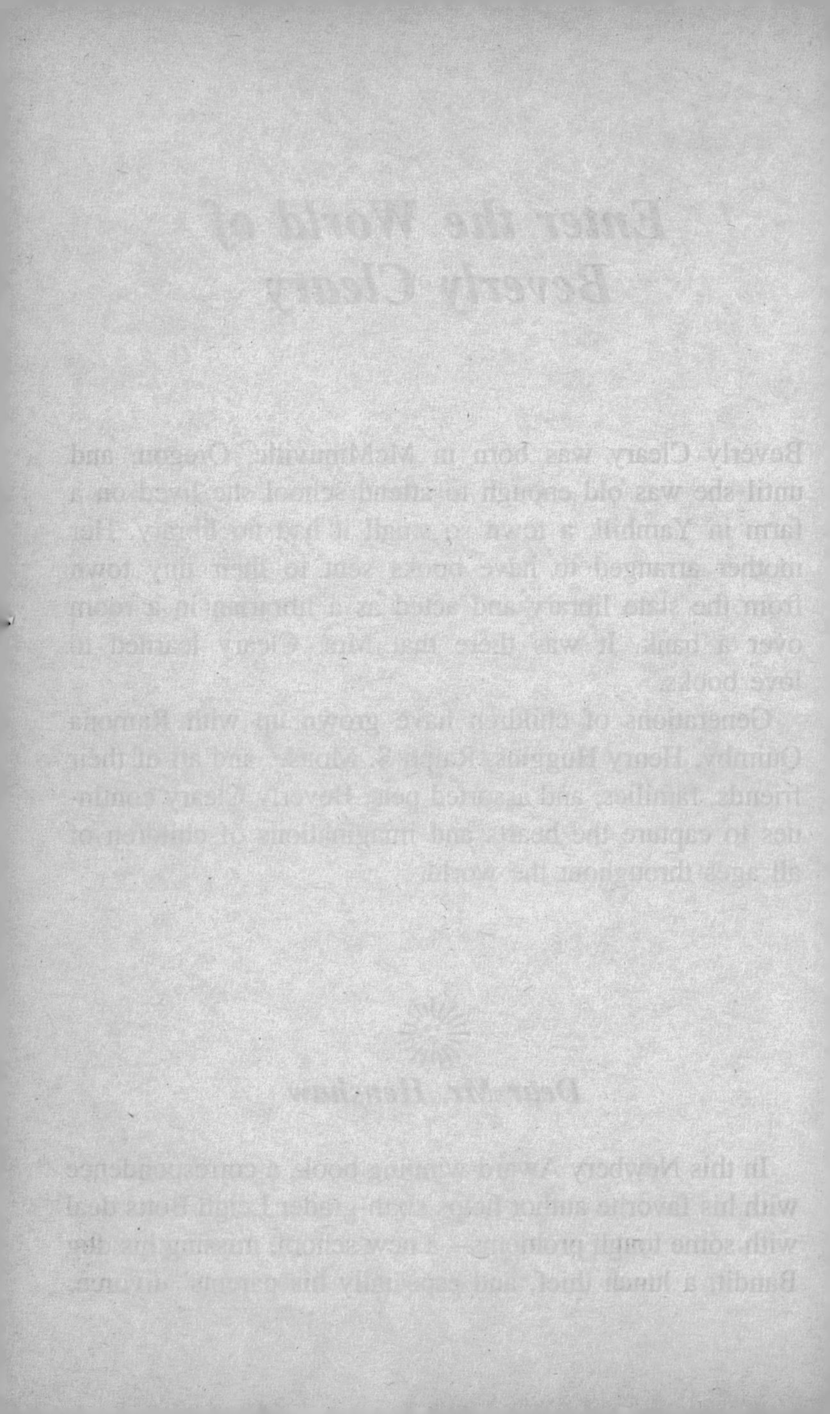

Enter the World of Beverly Cleary

Beverly Cleary was born in McMinnville, Oregon, and until she was old enough to attend school she lived on a farm in Yamhill, a town so small it had no library. Her mother arranged to have books sent to their tiny town from the state library and acted as a librarian in a room over a bank. It was there that Mrs. Cleary learned to love books.

Generations of children have grown up with Ramona Quimby, Henry Huggins, Ralph S. Mouse, and all of their friends, families, and assorted pets. Beverly Cleary continues to capture the hearts and imaginations of children of all ages throughout the world.

Dear Mr. Henshaw

In this Newbery Award-winning book, a correspondence with his favorite author helps sixth-grader Leigh Botts deal with some tough problems—a new school, missing his dog Bandit, a lunch thief, and especially his parents' divorce.

Strider

In the sequel to the Newbery winner *Dear Mr. Henshaw,* Leigh Botts is down in the dumps. His parents have divorced and his dog has run away, and it doesn't look as if things could get any worse. But Leigh's life takes a turn for the better when he adopts a stray dog named Strider.

Beezus and Ramona

Beezus tries very hard to be patient with her little sister, but four-year-old Ramona has a habit of doing the most unpredictable, annoying, embarrassing things in the world. Sometimes Beezus doesn't like Ramona much, and that makes her feel very guilty. Sisters are supposed to love each other, but pesky little Ramona doesn't seem very lovable to Beezus right now.

Ramona the Pest

Ramona is off to kindergarten, and it is the greatest day of her life. She loves her teacher, Miss Binney, and she likes a little boy named Davy so much she wants to kiss him. So why does Ramona get in so much trouble? And how does Ramona manage to disrupt the whole class during rest time? Anyone who knows Ramona knows that she never *tries* to be a pest.

Ramona the Brave

Now that she's six and entering the first grade, Ramona is determined to be brave, but it's not always easy, with a scary new all-by-herself bedroom, her mother's new job, and a new teacher who just doesn't understand how hard Ramona is trying to grow up.

Ramona and Her Father

In this Newbery Honor Book, the whole family is grumpy when Mr. Quimby loses his job. Ramona keeps trying to cheer up her family, but every new idea seems to cause more trouble. Her sister and parents, even her teacher, seem to have lost their patience with Ramona. But when her father tells her he wouldn't trade her for a million dollars, Ramona knows everything will be okay.

Ramona and Her Mother

When Ramona's mother takes on a full-time job, there's trouble in the Quimby household. Seven-and-a-half-year-old Ramona feels unloved and starts twitching her nose like a rabbit, until her teacher becomes concerned.

Ramona Quimby, Age 8

Ramona feels quite grown up taking the bus by herself, helping big sister Beezus make dinner, and trying hard to be nice to pesky Willa Jean after school. Turning eight years old and entering the third grade can do that to a girl. So how can her teacher call her a nuisance? Being a member of the Quimby family in the third grade is harder than Ramona expected.

Ramona Forever

From the moment Howie Kemp's mysterious "rich" Uncle Hobart arrives from Saudi Arabia, life becomes more and more confusing. What's so special about Uncle Hobart, who only teases Ramona? And why are Ramona's mother and Aunt Bea keeping secrets? Life for Ramona is full of beginnings, discoveries, and surprises. But through all of the happiness and change, and some small moments of sadness, she's always wonderful Ramona—forever!

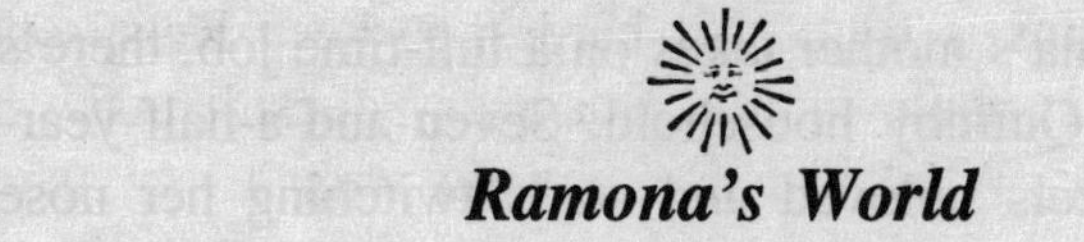

Ramona's World

Ramona is sure this will be "the best year of her life, so far." She can show off her calluses from swinging on the rings in the park. The boy she calls Yard Ape sits across the aisle from her in school. Her teacher, Mrs. Meacham, praises her writing. Best of all, she has Daisy, her new best friend. But little does Ramona know the challenges her fourth-grade year holds in store!

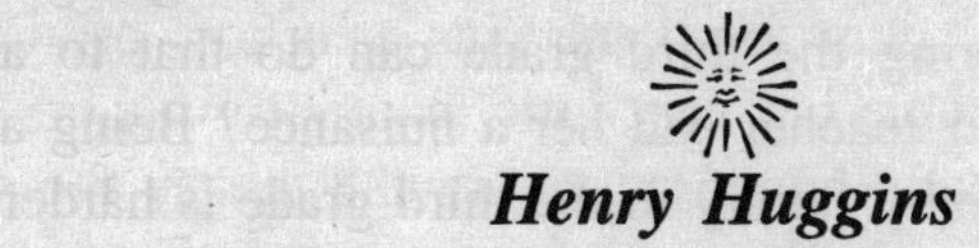

Henry Huggins

Henry Huggins feels that nothing very interesting ever happens to him. But from the moment a stray dog in the drugstore begs for a taste of his ice cream cone and downs it in one gulp, everything is different. Henry names the dog Ribsy and decides to keep him. And that's only the beginning of Henry's exciting new life!

Henry and Ribsy

Henry Huggins is trying his hardest to keep Ribsy out of trouble for a whole month. But Ribsy doesn't make it easy for Henry. What can one boy do with a dog who steals a policeman's lunch and an ice cream cone from Ramona Quimby?

Henry and Beezus

All Henry Huggins can think about is owning a bicycle, especially since that big show-off Scooter McCarthy has one. Selling bubble gum to all the kids at school brings Henry plenty of trouble but very little money for his bike fund. Can a girl really help Henry earn the money for a bicycle? Henry's friend Beezus helps him turn the most humiliating situation of his life into a real business success.

Henry and the Clubhouse

Henry Huggins has a lot of good ideas when he first begins his paper route, especially the idea to build a clubhouse. Henry and his friends don't want any girls hanging out at their new clubhouse. But a silly old sign that says NO GIRLS ALLOWED can't stop Beezus and Ramona Quimby.

Henry and the Paper Route

Henry Huggins couldn't wait to turn eleven years old so he could have a paper route like his friend Scooter. He was sure he could prove that he was responsible enough to handle the job. But Henry is sidetracked by four lively kittens, one boy with a robot, and Ramona Quimby, the ever-present pest of Klickitat Street.

Ribsy

Poor Ribsy! Somehow he's gotten himself hopelessly lost in a huge shopping mall parking lot. Even worse, he ends up in the wrong family's car. Ribsy doesn't want to live in a house where three girls give him a bubble bath. All he wants to do is go home and be Henry Huggins's dog again. Instead, he's about to begin the liveliest adventure of his life!

The Mouse and the Motorcycle

Ralph only wanted to ride the mouse-sized motorcycle someone had left on the table in the hotel room where Ralph lived. Instead, both Ralph and the motorcycle take a terrible fall into the wastepaper basket, where they are trapped until Keith, the owner of the motorcycle, rescues them. Keith teaches Ralph to ride the motorcycle, and the two of them soon find out that adventures can be both fun and dangerous!

Runaway Ralph

Ralph has made up his mind—he is going to run away. Envisioning fun, freedom, and delicious crumbs from peanut-butter-and-jelly sandwiches, he hops on his red bike and zooms away to the summer camp down the road. Once he arrives, he runs headlong into a strict watchdog, a mouse-hungry cat, and even more fur-raising escapades. Suddenly home doesn't seem like a bad place to be.

Ralph S. Mouse

When Ralph's home at the Mountain View Inn is overrun by rowdy mice who want to use his red motorcycle, he packs up his prized machine and moves to a new home—inside Irwin J. Sneed Elementary School!

Ellen Tebbits

Ellen Tebbits believes she would die of embarrassment if any of the girls at school were to learn her secret. Then she meets Austine Allen, a new girl in class who is hiding the very same secret. They become best friends immediately, until Ellen slaps Austine in the middle of a crowded school lunchroom!

Otis Spofford

There is nothing Otis Spofford likes better than stirring up a little excitement. Otis also loves to tease Ellen Tebbits—probably because Ellen is so neat and clean, and she never fails to become angry. One day Otis's teasing goes a little too far, and now he is worried—because Ellen isn't just angry . . . she's planning something.

Emily's Runaway Imagination

Adventure is pretty scarce in Pitchfork, Oregon, so Emily keeps herself amused bleaching Dad's old plow horse and feeding the hogs an occasional treat. Then she decides that Pitchfork needs a library—and making it happen is the perfect challenge for a girl with a runaway imagination.

Muggie Maggie

When Maggie Schultz arbitrarily decides cursive writing is not for her, her rebellion gets her into trouble. Then Maggie becomes the message monitor, but she can't figure out what the teacher's notes say. Suddenly, Maggie finds cursive interesting. How can she read people's letters if she can't read cursive?

Socks

It was Socks's lucky day when he went to live with the Brickers. He got all of the attention he wanted. But that was before the Brickers came home with a new baby. Suddenly a crying little bundle is getting all of the attention, and Socks feels as if he's been replaced. What Socks doesn't know is that the baby is getting bigger every day and soon he will be joining Socks in all kinds of fun and mischief!

Mitch and Amy

Mitch and Amy are always squabbling about something. They think being twins is fun, but that's about the only thing they have in common—until the school bully starts picking on Mitch and Amy, too. Now the twins agree about one thing, and they can't waste any more time fighting with each other.

Fifteen

It seems too good to be true. The most popular boy in school has asked Jane out—and she's never even dated before. Stan is tall and good-looking, friendly and hard-working—everything Jane ever dreamed of. But is she ready for this? With warmth, perceptiveness, and humor, Beverly Cleary chronicles the joys and worries of a girl's first crush.

Jean and Johnny

It should be the happiest moment of Jean's life—instead of the most embarrassing. Why couldn't she have been ready when the best-looking, most popular boy in school asked her to dance? Instead she is stepping all over his feet and is completely tongue-tied. Despite her family's warning about chasing the handsome Johnny Chessler, Jean has to learn from experience the perils of a one-sided romance.

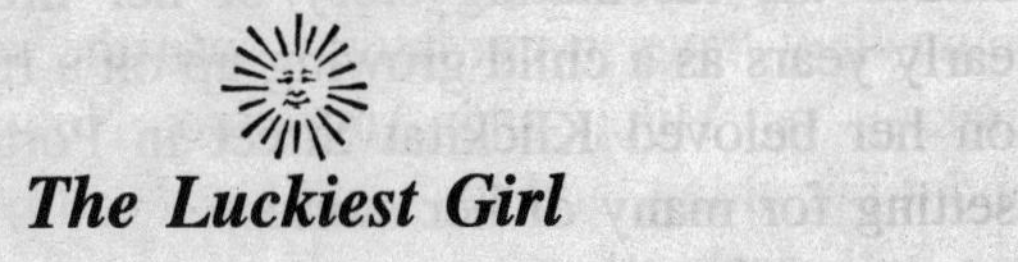

The Luckiest Girl

Shelley's spending the winter in California, and she feels as if she's living in a fantasyland. Now the star of the school basketball team is smiling at her, and all of the other girls are green with envy. Shelley feels like the luckiest girl in the world. She's about to discover the magic of falling in love—and a whole lot more!

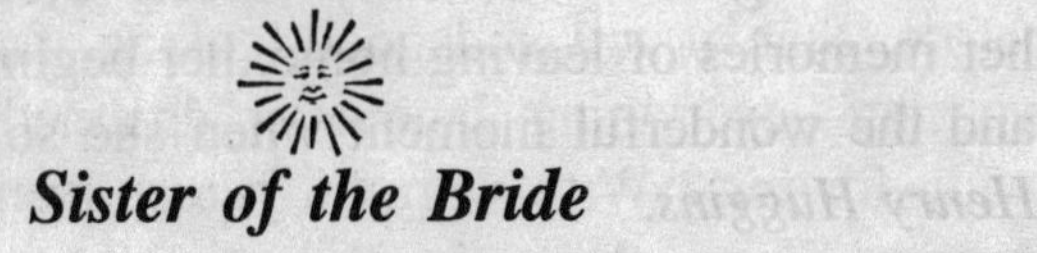

Sister of the Bride

Barbara can hardly believe her older sister is getting married. With all of the excitement, Barbara can't help dreaming of the day she will be the bride. But as the big day draws near and her sister turns suddenly apprehensive, the sister of the bride finds herself having second thoughts about running into love.

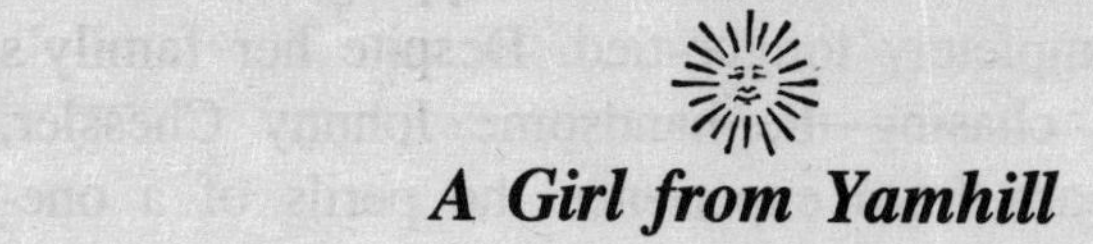

A Girl from Yamhill

In the first volume of her autobiography, Beverly Cleary shares the fascinating story of her life. She recalls her early years as a child growing up on a rural farm and later on her beloved Klickitat Street in Portland, Oregon, the setting for many of her stories.

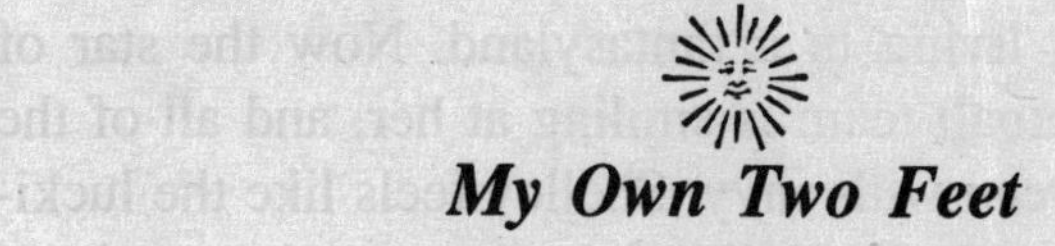

My Own Two Feet

The girl from Yamhill grows up. In the second volume of her autobiography, Beverly Cleary shares with her readers the origins of her early career. Cleary brings to life her memories of leaving home, her beginnings as a writer, and the wonderful moment when she sold her first book, *Henry Huggins.*